PEN PAL TALES

A collection by nine Leicester authors

Book Two, December 2025

Pen Pals Publishing

CONTENTS

DEDICATION AND ACKNOWLEDGEMENTS

To Guy Hodges, who contributed to *Pen Pal Tales: Book One* and was one of the original co-founders of Pen Pals Publishing. We miss his expertise in writing fantasy stories, and we look forward to his return soon.

Also, to Phil Tear (1954–2025), to whom *Book One* was dedicated. Phil was a great storyteller of Leicester and its people and is still greatly missed.

This second collection continues the spirit of both Guy and Phil — celebrating Leicester's voices, friendship, and the shared creativity that defines the Pen Pals journey.

And finally, a big thank you to all who have supported Pen Pals Publishing's grassroots initiative in turning our vision into reality: creating books that are accessible and affordable not only for writers but equally for readers.

WELCOME

Following the success of *Pen Pal Tales: Book One* (August 2025), **Pen Pals Publishing** proudly presents *Book Two Winter Edition* — a celebration of imagination, resilience, and community.

Like the first book, the writers featured here are ordinary people with wide and diverse life experiences that underpin their far-from-ordinary poems and stories. The shared theme of *winter* runs throughout this collection — a season of reflection, endurance, humour, and hope, explored through each author's unique perspective.

Within the "About the Authors" section, you'll also find "What Winter Means to Me", a short personal reflection from each contributor to help you connect with how winter resonates differently for every writer, and perhaps for you too.

Thank you to all the authors, each of whom has contributed not only their writing but also their time, ideas, and practical help in producing this anthology, and to the readers who continue to encourage our journey.

Thank you for joining us on this journey. If you've ever believed that stories belong to everyone, this book was made for you.

FOREWORD

By Dr Emma Astra (PhD), December 2025

When Pen Pals Publishing began, none of us knew quite what we were building—only that we wanted to write stories and make them accessible to friends and family. We wanted our writing to become something readers could hold, read, and share: an actual book or an easily accessed digital link. We were nine, now ten, ordinary writers from Leicester who loved words but had been given few opportunities and faced the usual gatekeeping barriers. What began as friends meeting in a creative writing class became a publishing collective with a shared belief: that writing (and reading) should be accessible, affordable, and authentic for everyone.

This Winter 2025 anthology, *Pen Pal Tales Book Two*, continues the path we began last summer. Our theme this time is winter—a season that can mean endurance, reflection, celebration, or simply the cold reality of getting through. Each author interprets it differently, from comic realism to fantasy, from memory to myth. Yet one thread runs through every page: warmth found in community.

A Word About Collectiveness

Each *Pen Pal Tales* book opens with a Foreword written by a different author or contributor, giving every publication its own voice. Our first Foreword was written by Les Dowse, whose eloquence beautifully captured our beginnings. This time, I am writing it. My words cannot match Les's rich vocabulary, but I want to honour the equal contribution of every co-founder.

When the group surprised me with a card, gifts, and a small ceremony marking my role in collating and managing the technical side, I was more touched than at my PhD graduation. But that sense of honour belongs to all of us.

Every co-founder has given their time, energy, and

creativity to make these books possible—not only through their writing but through the whole publishing process:

1. Anne Connue (pen name)
2. Terry Dickson
3. Les Dowse
4. Sheila Mayor
5. Malcolm Nez (pen name)
6. Tony O'Dwyer
7. Maria Irina Popescu (known as Irina Popescu)
8. Rosemary Watson
9. Guy Hodges
10. Emma Astra (full name: Emma Astra Aldwinckle)

We come from all walks of life—teachers, scientists, detectives, artists, parents, retirees, and researchers. None of us has agents or large literary networks; what we have is commitment, humour, and belief in each other. And of course, stories.

What We Do and Why

Pen Pals Publishing exists to open doors for writers who might otherwise remain unheard. Our model is simple: we share skills, publish together, and learn as we go, using our strengths and resources to achieve publication.

I prefer the word *collator* or *co-ordinator* to *editor*. Traditional editorial models can create hierarchy or distance; what we practise is creative democracy, offering authors the chance to contribute their skills to the process. Tony designs our covers; "Anne" crafts elegant prose and proofreads; Les provides precise editing and a vast vocabulary; Sheila brings memory and warmth; Terry adds moral storytelling and practical wisdom; "Malcolm" contributes scientific insight; Rosemary writes fables of empathy; Maria-Irina blends politics and poetry. I collate everything as my technology skills and understanding of publishing grow. Together, we weave our writing through research, lived experience, and storytelling. Everyone contributes; everyone matters. Everyone is equal; we would not have a book without any of our authors.

The Stories You'll Find Here
This book gathers our voices around one winter table:
Anne Connue writes two tender, witty re-imaginings of the Nativity.
Terry Dickson contrasts a modern-day Christmas miracle with a mischievous children's tale.
Les Dowse brings dialect poetry, satire, and moral drama in *Season of Goodwill*.
Sheila Mayor offers a vivid 1960s Scotland memoir full of kindness and connection.
Malcolm Nez contributes two pieces: *The Cyclist's Villanelle* and *In a Spin*, where roadside peril leads to communal joy and an unforgettable "Strip the Willow" dance.
Tony O'Dwyer writes *A Brush with Marilyn*, a witty art-world fantasy where celebrity meets chaos.
Maria-Irina Popescu mixes myth and politics in *Vampire Revolution*, set in revolutionary Romania.
Rosemary Watson explores transformation—from birds and witches to Richard III's ghost.
Emma Astra offers *Tales from the Hospital Ward*, darkly comic snapshots of hospital life in Leicester.

You may not love every story, but somewhere here may be one that speaks directly to you. Reading, like food or music, is a matter of taste. We aim to offer enough variety that everyone finds something nourishing for the soul.

Printer and Bookseller
Amazon's print-on-demand system has enabled us to publish high-quality paperbacks and e-books without any upfront costs —an essential resource for a grassroots community group with limited funding. For us, Amazon currently functions as both printer and bookseller, offering professional presentation, international availability, and the kind of accessibility once possible only through major publishing houses.

We remain open to exploring feasible opportunities with ethical publishers or local printers who share our values. Any future partnership must protect our authentic storytelling, keep costs affordable for writers and readers, and avoid upfront fees for authors.

Our Values and Vision

Pen Pals Publishing stands on three pillars: Accessibility, Affordability, and Authenticity—for both readers and writers.

We want books that everyone can afford, hold, hear, or download. We format every edition for paperback and Kindle e-Book, and we hope to expand into audiobooks to reduce exclusion. We also champion authenticity: real voices, not polished stereotypes.

As we grow, we plan to explore environmentally friendly printing and deepen our connection to Leicester's creative heritage. We draw inspiration from Leicester's proud printing history—from Toni Savage's *Phoenix Broadsheets* and *New Broom Press*, which helped launch the careers of writers like Spike Milligan and Sue Townsend. Savage reportedly ran his publishing operation from a Leicester bedsit, proving what can be achieved with limited resources.

Once a city of presses and paper, Leicester could again become a hub of inclusive, digital-age publishing—merging heritage with new technologies, including AI, to empower emerging writers and create greener books.

Pen Pals is exploring funding opportunities to offer free author copies, community workshops, and technological and accessibility innovations. A small grant or sponsor could help us reach more readers and teach others how to publish their own work.

No co-founder or contributor makes any money from this project; each has given their time, effort, and stories freely. Any future income will be reinvested to ensure sustainability and support Leicester-based charities.

For Readers and Future Writers

Pen Pals Publishing isn't just a group—it's a community movement for creativity. We aim to release a general anthology each summer and winter, plus special themed editions.

We warmly welcome submissions for future volumes. Co-founders may continue contributing and will always be listed as co-founders, guiding the collective's strategy even when not submitting work.

New writers—or those who help with the publishing process joining future books will not be co-founders but are encouraged to contribute skills such as editing, design, proofreading, outreach, and, of course, their valuable stories for publication.

We especially welcome writers who, for any reason, find it difficult to reach traditional publishers. Ideally, contributors will have some connection to Leicester—whether through living here, visiting, studying, or being inspired by the city's character.

Dreaming Small yet Big

Our dream is simple: to make it easy to buy, read, and share affordable books that celebrate real people, without gatekeeping. We always set our books at the lowest price Amazon allows, recognising the financial pressures faced by readers worldwide. Any future developments will reinvest funds directly into Pen Pals Publishing, with the long-term aim of becoming a Community Interest Company or a similar not-for-profit model.

Our Mission and Thanks

To our readers: thank you. You are part of this story. Without you, words stay in drawers; with you, they come alive.

Our mission is to make reading joyful —to remind people that literature is not an exam but a conversation. Leicester is a city of underdogs who rise; look at the football team's 2016 miracle. We carry that same belief: that with courage, creativity, and community, anyone can make it.

Just as with food or TV, what one person loves, another may not. Our anthologies span different genres and styles, so every reader can find something that suits their taste.

So light a candle, pour a drink, or curl up beneath a blanket this winter as you read this book. Some stories may make you laugh; others may move you to tears—but all were written with sincerity, humour, and hope. Each page is a spark in the winter dark, a reminder that stories can warm the world.

From the co-founders of Pen Pals Publishing—equal partners, friends, and storytellers—we thank you for reading, believing, and helping grassroots publishing grow.

Updates and contact information:
www.linktr.ee/penpalspublishing

TWO STORIES
By
Anne Connue

Above image was created using AI

A WINTER'S JOURNEY

A few months ago, my sister visited me. She's the widow of a rich man and lives in Galilee. She told me about a radical young preacher who was crucified a few months ago.

'He called himself the Son of God,' she said. I remembered yet again my long-ago journey to see the newborn child in the stable: "The Saviour who is the Messiah...."

I've never forgotten that journey. It was a freezing winter's night. Me and the lads were out on the hills with the sheep as we always were at that time of the year. Some of the ewes weren't far off lambing, so we'd put them into the fold to keep an eye on them, and the rest of the flock was grazing nearby. We huddled around the fire and talked about the census and the travellers coming to the town in the valley to register their names. We'd already been and done it. Jacob grumbled about it being a complete waste of time. Sam snored, and Dan was silent, lying on his back, gazing at the stars. I know nowt' about them, but they were beautiful that night against a clear sky.

Then Dan said, 'What's that noise?'

'Jacob and Sam.'

'No. Listen. Sam, wake up! And look... that light!'

Jacob and Sam said nothing, but Sam struggled onto one elbow. We looked in the direction Dan was pointing. The light was brighter than any I've seen before or since. There was singing and an unearthly voice spoke: '...to you is born this day in the City of David a Saviour who is the Messiah... you shall find him wrapped in swaddling bands and lying in a manger... Glory to God in the highest...'

'Come on,' I said. There was no question of anyone remaining behind. We closed the gate on the pregnant ewes and trusted that the dogs and the fires would keep marauding animals away from the flock. Then we pulled our cloaks round us and set off down the hill towards the town.

'That voice, the one that said "The City of David". Does that mean our town?', said Dan.

'Aye, 'ave you never heard it called so?' asked Sam, wide awake now.

'Me granddad mentioned it that last time I saw him,' but I've never heard nowt' else,' admitted Dan. He was about fourteen, a good lad and a hard worker, but lacking in education.

The path led between trees as it approached the town, and I could hear Jacob grumbling behind me:

'This path will be the death of us, so it will!'

'Never mind, Jacob,' soothed Sam. 'Not far now. Take my arm.'

'And how are we to find this child in swaddling bands? All babes are wrapped in swaddling bands!'

'Well, he's lying in a manger, and I don't suppose there are many babes in a cowshed at this time of year, so I expect we'll come across him soon,' said Sam.

Presently, we arrived at the market square to find it was jammed with people, despite the lateness of the hour. 'Let's hope we can find this babe amongst all the travellers come for the census,' muttered Jacob. He turned to me: 'So, Reuben, where to now?'

I had no idea. We were cold and hungry, and I was beginning to worry about the sheep. Had we made a mistake? We were all silent for a moment.

Then Dan exclaimed, 'That way! Over there! Where that star is!'

He was pointing towards a large star shining over a street behind the square. Even now, I don't know how he knew that the star was important. He hurried towards it and, for want of anything better, we followed him, treading through dirt, elbowing our way past food sellers, travellers, pedlars, soldiers, beggars and whores, all shouting their wares. Dan pushed a girl with red hair and an ample bosom out of the way and dived down a side street. An inn called The Kings of the East appeared to be

13

doing a good trade, and low above the roof, hung the bright star. A muddy path led from the street to a stable at the back, and as we peered inside, I suddenly knew this was the place we sought —the end of our journey.

It was warm and quiet, and the noise and dirt of the town were no more than a memory as we crept forward to see the child in the manger. Suddenly, we were no longer cold and annoyed.

Instead, we were entranced by this baby boy, his dark eyes peering solemnly from beneath a thatch of black hair, his limbs swaddled as all babies were. He seemed an ordinary boy, but he was not, and we could not take our eyes from him... a Saviour who is the Messiah... We had all grown up learning that one day the Messiah would come, and now this was he. His mother and father, ordinary people, like us, sat and watched; she was very young, he a good deal older. Even the oxen and the ass were watching, and we somehow knew they, too, were protecting this child.

We returned to the hills, and later we heard a rumour that three kings had come to the town to visit the baby in the stable. Then there was more gossip that the child and his parents had disappeared; no one knew where or why.

It all happened over thirty years ago, but I cannot forget it, nor the story my sister told me about the young preacher who was crucified.

Anne Connue

GABRIELLE'S MISSION

'Are you getting broody in your old age? Or simply suffering from one of your periodic bouts of madness?' asked Gabrielle.

She glared at The Boss. He had summoned her to the Viewing Gallery to tell her he wanted to send her on a Mission. This was not unusual. She was one of the four chief Messengers in his organisation and the only female who worked for him. The Boss was Almighty, Omnipotent and Creative, worshipped and adored by millions of his people, but he never went anywhere. He didn't need to. If he wanted one of his people to do something, it was the Messengers' job to make sure that something was done.

Usually, Gabrielle was happy to do whatever he asked her. But every so often, he appeared to go out of his mind, and when he did, she felt it to be her duty to bring him back to sanity. This was one of those times.

'I'm neither mad nor broody,' he said calmly. 'And I know exactly what I'm doing.'

'Oh, yes?'

She cut him short, too angry to let him finish.

'That was what you said when you told that family – what were they called? Noah was to build that crazy, smelly boat and take all those animals on board. And then you drowned everyone and everything else! And what about that poor man Job? You robbed him of all he held dear, and when he complained, you told him to keep quiet because you'd created the heavens! And now you're saying that you want a son and you expect me to go down there to tell a sixteen-year-old *virgin* that she's pregnant?'

Gabrielle had to stop talking because she'd run out of breath.

'Have you finished?' asked The Boss.

She scowled at him, and he said, 'If you think you can't manage it, I'll send Mike or Rafe or Uri instead.'

His dark eyes twinkled beneath his bushy eyebrows, but Gabrielle was too cross to notice.

'Of course I can manage it! But aren't you forgetting something?'

'I don't think so. What?'

'Well, if she's a *virgin*, she can't be pregnant, can she?' Gabrielle reminded him triumphantly. 'In case you've forgotten, it takes a woman *and* a man to make a baby!'

'Really? Remind me.'

'Well... they have to... you know...'

'No.'

There was silence. Then The Boss, who was short and stocky and black, laughed. He never doubted that she would be the best Messenger for this Mission. Suddenly, Gabrielle's anger ebbed away, and she laughed too.

'I hope you never let one of the People fool you the way I do!' said The Boss. 'Don't worry: the Spirit will do what is necessary.'

'But the girl,' protested Gabrielle. 'What about her?'

'Look,' said The Boss. He turned to the world, far below the Viewing Gallery and pointed to the land he called Palestine.

'There she is. See? Down there by the well, wearing the blue robe. With the man in grey.'

Gabrielle looked. She herself was slim and immensely tall, with a cloak of blonde hair that swirled around her as she moved and huge violet eyes that flashed fire when she was angry. The girl they were observing was buxom and lively, with long dark hair, like all the other girls in that neighbourhood. She was laughing at something the man in grey was saying. He had a beard and seemed a good deal older than the girl.

'What's her name? And his?' asked Gabrielle.

'She's Mary, and his name is Joseph. He's her fiancé.'

This was news to Gabrielle. 'Her *what*?'

'Gabrielle, just have faith in me. Believe me, I know what I'm doing. First, let me tell you what I want you to say to Mary. And when you've visited her, come back here and I will give you fresh instructions because I shall want you to visit Joseph...'

And that was how the most important Mission of Gabrielle's career began. But there was still one thing that puzzled her. As she was about to go out through The Gates, she said to The Boss: 'One more question, Boss. Why? I can understand that you might want a son, but why like this?'

'Because My People are in danger of losing their way. One day, My Son will show them how to find it. '

As he spoke, he looked sad. Gabrielle wondered why, but didn't ask.

Whilst Gabrielle was away, The Boss spent a good deal of time watching her from the Viewing Gallery. He heard her talking to Mary: 'Do not be afraid, the Lord is with thee...'

'Good girl,' he murmured approvingly. He remembered what she had said to him earlier about the Noah family and Job. She never minced her words, and he didn't blame her for that. But she didn't understand. None of them did. And sometimes that worried him.

When Gabrielle returned, The Boss asked her: 'Well?'

'Very well,' said Gabrielle. 'Just as you said.'

She beamed at him, and he smiled back and said nothing. Instead, once again, he beckoned her to the Gallery. Again, they saw Mary talking to Joseph, but this time Mary looked unhappy and:

'He's furious,' said The Boss.

Gabrielle was irritated. 'Well, of course he is! What do you expect? He thinks she's played him false!'

'He's not a bad man,' said The Boss. 'But he's proud. He won't stand being made a fool of. He's descended from King David, did you know? He's already thinking about putting Mary aside, quietly and without a fuss. And that's where you come in. You need to go to him and persuade him to go ahead with the marriage. I'll leave it to you how you do it.'

Gabrielle was astonished. This was an honour and a great responsibility. To persuade this man to marry the girl who was

17

carrying The Boss's son! And to choose her own way of doing it.

Again, The Boss watched and listened. Gabrielle, looking stunningly beautiful (the hussy!), reminded Joseph that as a good Jew, he should obey the wishes of The Boss. And what The Boss wanted was that Joseph should marry Mary.

Simple. Joseph was soft clay in Gabrielle's hands, and The Boss, deeply appreciative of her tactics, admitted that Uri or Rafe or Mike would never have succeeded half as well. He laughed to himself as she left Joseph and came back to the Gallery.

'Easy!' she told him, pleased with herself.

'So, I saw,' he said drily. 'Now watch.'

It seemed only a moment later that a heavily pregnant Mary was accompanying Joseph on a journey.

'They have to go to Bethlehem – Joseph was born there and now he must return there with his wife to take part in the census,' explained The Boss.

'It's a pity the census can't take place at Mary's home,' commented Gabrielle. 'There's no room at the inn, and she's nine months gone. I expect she's exhausted after the journey, and the only place they can find to stay is a stable! Do you want her to miscarry?'

'Hush! ... Wait ... Look, there is My Son... all your worries are for nothing...'

Somehow, time had moved on. Gabrielle was silent, immensely moved.

'Boss... he - he's beautiful... peaceful ... he's lovely! And she's so calm and serene! And Joseph: what must he be feeling?'

Gabrielle was absorbed in the sight of the three people in the stable. Then, in the distance, she heard a familiar sound.

'Is that the Choir? They're good tonight! Where are they singing?'

'Over there ...' said The Boss. Gabrielle looked along the line of his pointing finger. 'The men in the fields below are shepherds. The Choir are telling them about my Son and they will go to visit him.'

Gabrielle listened, her head on one side. The Choir was another branch of The Organisation. She had sung with them for a long time before she became a Messenger, and she knew many of the Choristers. Finally, they fell silent, and the shepherds hurried off to visit The Boss's Son.

'See those other visitors?' said The Boss presently. He pointed to three richly dressed men, laden with precious gifts, making slow progress from the East. They seemed to be following a star. When they arrived at Jerusalem, they stopped.

'Now what?' asked Gabrielle. 'They won't find your son there'

'They don't know that. They're looking for the new King of the Jews. What they have found instead is King Herod: a nasty piece of work. Listen to him inviting them back when they have found the baby king... No, Herod, you do *not* wish to worship My Son, and you will *not* be seeing these visitors again.'

The Boss swung round and spoke to Gabrielle, urgently. 'Gabrielle, those three visitors are good men, but on no account must they be allowed to visit Jerusalem when they return to their own lands. You must warn them. And when you have spoken to them, you must tell Joseph to take Mary and the child to Egypt to avoid the wrath of Herod.'

Gabrielle looked startled. 'Go!' barked The Boss. 'There's no time to lose! This is important!'

Gabrielle jumped. The Boss had never spoken to her like this before.

' I'm going, Boss! I won't fail you, I promise! *Don't worry!*'

She was gone, in a swirl of hair.

The Boss didn't doubt Gabrielle's ability to do as he asked. But he still worried. What would she say and how would she feel when she found out what was to come?

Anne Connue

TWO STORIES
By
Terry Dickson

BEN

It had been two days since he saw his picture again on a Leicester Mercury newsstand. The photograph showed him suntanned, grinning and with a crew cut. It was unlikely that anyone would recognise him from it. After three weeks of sleeping rough, eleven-year-old Ben's face is thin and drawn. A green woollen hat, pulled over his now-long black hair, accentuates his pale skin and deep blue eyes. A black parka tops off his layers of clothing. He has learned to walk purposefully in public view. Boys of his age draw attention if they appear to be wandering or lost. Normally, he keeps out of sight during school hours, but it's the Christmas holiday, so he doesn't have to worry.

The city centre is noisy, cold and busy. Leaving it behind, Ben makes for Abbey Meadow Mills. The industrial estate is home to a selection of abandoned factories. The buildings, in their dilapidated state, are ideal for rough sleepers. Ben has found a place there where he feels safe. In the undergrowth at the bottom of a slope is a window into a basement. The main door has been bricked up. Pulling an old piece of plywood across the dirty window hides it from view. The room is dry and relatively clean; a few wooden pallets are stacked along one wall. A big cupboard with a strong door is Ben's hideout. Approaching the basement, he lies down in the undergrowth and waits. He fears being followed back to his safe place.

Lying in the dark, Ben can see Christmas lights shining in distant houses. He hears the River Soar running nearby. Living on the streets was frightening at first, but he is bright and has adapted as best he can. The money he saved towards a new bike is running low, so he spends as little as possible on food.

Satisfied that he has not been followed, Ben moves down the slope. Pulling back the plywood, torch in hand, he squeezes himself inside. He hears a woman's soft voice say

'Hello.'

Frightened, Ben pulls the board back, ready to make his escape.

'Please don't run,' she says.

Something in her voice calms him.

'Who are you, what do you want?'

In the light of his torch, he sees a small lady, swathed in bright coloured clothes, with white hair sticking out the sides of a red woollen hat. Her chubby face is lit up by a beaming smile and vivid blue eyes, a bit like his. A nylon shopping bag lies beside her.

'I live the same way that you do. It's Christmas Eve, and I just wanted to spend it with someone. I had a good day today, and I've got too much food for one, maybe we could share it. My name is Geraldine.'

'I'm Ben. Is it really Christmas Eve?'

Ben, nervous at first, sits down on some pallets near Geraldine. She pulls food from the bag: sausage rolls, sandwiches, mince pies and chocolate biscuits. She even has a flask full of hot chocolate. He is so hungry; they sit eating the tasty food. She puts an old-fashioned square bicycle light on the pallets. The chocolate drink tastes wonderful. As he eats, he begins to relax.

'You really are far too young to be living like this, Ben. You must have been very unhappy at home.'

'Ah didn't know what else to do, ah was frightened at home.'

'Oh.'

'There is only mum and her boyfriend there. He's called Alan, and he's in the Army. When he first moved in, he was really good to us. We got on well and we were happy. He used to take me fishing, and it was great. Then he got sent to Afghanistan, and he changed.'

'How did he change Ben?'

'He wasn't nice to us any more, shouting at us for nothing. Ah, got worried he would hit us; his temper is terrible. He used to be really funny. Then he started drinking, and it made him worse.'

'Do you think Alan might be ill, Ben?'

'Mum kept on at him to go doctors, ah think he's on tablets

23

now. He still frightens me.'

'What an awful situation.'

'It's made my mum ill, she's on tablets as well, for depression.'

'What are you going to do in the long term, dear?'

'Ah don't know, ah can't help my mum, ah can't protect her or anything. Ah don't like being away from her, but ah don't know what else ah can do. Ahm frightened all the time.'

'What do you think would happen if you went home?'

'Ah, don't know how well my mum is. If she couldn't look after me, ah would finish up in one of them kid's homes,' says Ben.

'Have you got any relatives who could tell you how your mum is?'

'No, not since my nan died over a year ago. Ah keep wantin to ring mum, ah know she will be worried. If ah heard her voice, I would go straight home, and things would be the same.'

'How did you find this place?'

'Alan brought me here once fishing, and ah saw the empty buildings. Ah got a bus to Abbey Park, ah knew it was near here.'

'Oh, dear Ben, you shouldn't have all this worry at such a young age,' says Geraldine.

'Ah know, ah don't know what to do.'

Ben shows Geraldine a thick, glossy animal encyclopedia he found in a skip. He is very knowledgeable about animals and shares that knowledge with her. She listens patiently, pleased that he has momentarily forgotten his plight. In a while, they both begin to yawn, drowsy after lots of food and hot drinks. It was time to sleep. Geraldine begins unrolling her sleeping bag, and Ben heads towards his cupboard.

'Goodnight, Geraldine, thank you for the food, it was smashing,' he says.

'Goodnight, Benny Bear.'

Just as he drifts off to a warm, contented sleep, he realises that she called him Benny Bear. The only person who had ever called him that was his nan. Also, no matter how much hot chocolate they poured from the flask, it never emptied.

The next morning, Ben is startled by a knock on the cupboard door.

'Who is it?'

He is pulling on his shoes so that he can run if he has to.

'It's Geraldine, can you come outside with me? There's something I want you to see.'

Fuzzy with sleep, Ben gets dressed and stumbles out into the basement.

'Have a look outside,' says Geraldine.

Ben pulls the board aside and looks out. Overcome by emotion, he doesn't know what to do, laugh, cheer, shout or scream. The boy stands still, shaking and sobbing.

His mother, Alice, is standing on the road a few yards away. She is smiling and crying at the same time. She looks really pretty in her favourite blue corduroy coat. Tears cloud Ben's eyes as he clambers out of the window and runs into her arms. They weep, clinging to each other.

Alice tells him that Alan's brother has taken him to Manchester to look after him permanently. She tells Ben how much she has missed him.

'How did you find me, mum?', he said, still sniffling.

'An old lady came to the house last night and said that she knew where you were. I didn't believe her at first. Then she told me so many details about you that I thought it must be true. She arranged to pick me up in a taxi this morning, and here I am.'

'What did the lady look like?'

'She's little, with white hair and a lovely face. She said her name was Geraldine. She's in the taxi.'

'I must go and thank her mum.'

Ben goes to the taxi; he can see that she isn't in it. He returns to the basement; she isn't there either, nor is her shopping bag. He wonders how she could have left without being seen. The only trace of Geraldine is the red woollen hat, which he picks up.

Puzzled and excited, he goes back out to his mum; they get into the taxi.

'Let's get you back home where you belong. You are the best Christmas present ever,' said Alice, still hugging him.

The taxi pulls away as Ben sits clutching the red hat. Mother and son start discussing who Geraldine was and how on earth she had managed to reunite them. The taxi driver could hear their conversation, laughing, he said –

'Blimey, haven't you two ever heard of the Christmas fairy?'

Terry Dickson

BOWRITE AND THE
SEVEN ORFES
500 Words for kids

Once upon a time, a boy called Bowrite lived with his cruel stepmother Esmerelda. She scolded him constantly and treated him as a slave. Bowrite liked to escape to a little pond and feed worms to the seven beautiful Golden Orfe fish. His friend Con Thumb, the Irish imp, came with him. Esmerlda fell in love with a handsome Knight who wanted to marry her, but he didn't want Bowrite. Esmerelda went to the local witch, who gave her a poisoned apple that would make the boy sleep forever. Bowrite ate the apple and fell asleep in the cold attic that night; he didn't wake up. Esmerelda married the Knight and moved to his Land.

Con visited his friend and could tell that he was under a spell. The imp knew the Orfes' secret and went to them for help. He explained Bowrite's plight to Pusch Orfe, their leader. He told Con that he must find out how to break the spell. The Orfes changed into their other form, that of dwarves. Clad in red leather and blue hats, they had rosy cheeks and white beards. They went to the house and watched over their friend to keep him safe until he woke.

Con went to see the witch, begging her to lift the spell on Bowrite, but she said it was impossible. He asked how the spell could be broken, but she refused to tell him.

After weeks of pestering and begging her, she finally told Con,

'His brow must be wiped with the giant's snot.'

The fearsome giant called Thragar lived in a cave in the next valley. He was known to steal dogs and sheep and eat them whole. Con related this to Pusch, who thought of a plan; they gathered some items and set off.

The fearless band reached the cave in the dead of night. A dreadful snoring echoed from within; a big torch burned inside. They all crept inside. Thargar was lying flat on his back. Con climbed onto the giant's massive chest, and the rising and falling of it made it difficult for him to balance. He unfolded a bedsheet; two dwarves stood on either side of the great head and held it close to his nose. Con was then passed a sack of pepper and a large spoon. The imp then threw spoonfuls of the pepper into the huge nostrils. The giant took a deep breath, and his nose twitched. The two dwarves holding the sheet braced themselves as Thargar let out a powerful sneeze. The force of it sent Con rolling down onto the floor. The sheet was dragged away, covered in sticky snot. The giant sat up and roared as the dwarves ran from the cave, picking little Con up on the way.

Excitedly, the group watched as Pusch rubbed some snot onto Bowrite's forehead; the boy woke immediately. Everyone danced and sang with delight.

The dwarves returned to their peaceful life in the pond. Bowrite and Con lived happily ever after.

Terry Dickson

THREE POEMS AND A STORY
By
Les Dowse

1960'S SATDI NITE 'UNTIN'

It's Satdi nite an' ah feel like dancin',
So off to t'Palais to do some prancin'.
Wearin' me best blue mo'air suit –
Three button jacket, tight pants – what a beaut!

Ah rock up there 'bout 'alf pas' nine.
Look at them chicks! They could all be mine!
Watch 'em movin' around the floor,
There's one fer me, of that ah'm sure.

First things first, so ah get me a drink.
Study the girls an' 'ave a good think.
Whichever lucky girl ah choose,
It won't be becos she's got dancin' shoes.

Ya never pick from the prettiest.
Too self-centred! Select from the rest.
When you choose one she'll be so keen,
Putty in yor 'ands, know wha' ah mean?

After the last waltz ah tek 'er 'ome,
Snugglin' up like a dog wi' a bone.
She feels so good, she couldn't be keener
An' she can't wait to get in me Ford Cortina.

We'll park on the way, without discussions,
An' soon we'll be on the back seat cushions.
An' if ah get all that ah seek,
Ah might tek 'er to the pictures mid-week.

Les Dowse

CERTAINTY

My dog and I are happy now,

Watching the stream swirling below.

The ice has gone;

The fields are free from snow.

Somewhere a bird sings wildly,

Desperate to be heard.

'Soon, soon, Springtime is coming,'

Sings the bird.

Les Dowse

CHRISTMAS — OLD SCHOOL

Christmas morning when I were young:
'ouse full o' people, nigh a score,
Christmas carols, tunelessly sung,
Uncle Eric on the floor.
(Coughing up 'is lung).

In the kitchen, steamed-up winders;
Wimmen running around like rats;
Roasted 'taters, crisp as cinders,
Turkey, tough as wings on bats.
(Thank you Findus).

Christmas pudding on the table,
People slavering around it
Like gargoyles on church's gable,
Demons from 'ell's deepest pit.
(Like cousin Abel).

Christmas Day in the afternoon,
Bodies slumped, noisy digestion;
The Queen's speech'll not rouse 'em soon.
What comes next? That's the question.
(Tea time – that's what).

Sandwiches o' turkey remnants;
Sherry trifle, spicy mince pies;
Christmas cake to stretch yer pants;
Shitty crackers – no surprise!
(Crappy contents).

After tea the men get bladdered.
The ladies get genteely "lit".
Make-up's smudged, stockings laddered.
Bloated kids create cesspit.
(On bathroom floor).

After New Year, all year long,
People fondly think o' Christmas.
Me, I sing a different song.
I pray for the year to pass.
(Without Noel).

Les Dowse

SEASON OF GOODWILL

Rodric Loach came up from the east. From that flat, sodden land which, to the people of the villages on the Heath, seemed to stretch away endlessly, beyond the horizon. A land scattered with lakes peering out of the tangled woodland and scrub cover, penetrated by tidal creeks and a network of wide, arrow-straight waterways, much silted up nowadays, which had been constructed so long ago that only God knew by whom and for what purpose. No one remembered that the region had once been a vast, fertile plain until the sea level began to rise a couple of centuries ago, flooding the fair land with its salty torrent.

He arrived on the Heath one cold morning at Summer's end, the sun poking its nose through the odd hole in the cloud cover and the overnight frost still lingering in shaded places. The village he came to was called Skinton by its inhabitants, an erosion over the centuries of its original name of Skillington - the settlement of Scilla's people two thousand years past. He brought the heavily-laden, horse-drawn wagon to a halt on the bridge over the stream that bisected the village. An old man stood looking down at the moorhens searching for food among the reeds and water irises in the water below. Roddi Loach climbed down from the wagon.

'Morning to ya,' he said to the old man. The old man looked him up and down, taking in Roddi's scrawny body, bandy legs, narrow, feral eyes and long hair pulled back into a ponytail.
    'Not from round 'ere, are yeh?' he said, thinking to himself, "Wetlander! One of that bloody tribe!" The gold earring and the tattoo on Roddi's neck added weight to this judgment.
    'That's true, I'm not local. I'm a traveller looking for a place to settle down. And this looks a nice sort o' place.'
    'We think it is,' said the old man, spitting into the stream, 'but strangers might not find it so friendly. Depends, o' course, on

'ow they be'aves themselves.'

'Quite right,' said Roddi. 'You don't want no troublemakers around the place. I'm quiet an' law abiding meself.'

'If you're lookin' to start farmin', all the land round this village is taken up already. You'd best be lookin' elsewhere,' said the old man meaningfully.

'I'm not a farmer. All I need is somewhere to set meself up. I noticed half the houses are empty, some falling down. Reckon I could find somewhere to suit me purposes without too much trouble.'

'What's your trade, then?'

'I'm what you might call an apothecary-medicines, pills an' potions an' the like,' said Roddi.

'Well, we ain't got one o' them round 'ere as I knows of,' said the old man. 'You'll be travellin' all over the neighbour'ood, I suppose.

'Once I get set up ,' said Roddi, 'I'll be out an' about.'

Later that day Roddi Loach decided that an abandoned Methodist chapel on the village's back street was well suited to his needs. Having ascertained from its nearest neighbours that no one owned the building, he unhitched the wagon, fed his horse and carried his stuff inside. At that time of day nearly everyone was at work and so there was no inquisitive crowd to watch him move in. If there had been, the purpose of the large metal container with its stand, incorporating a firebox, would have engendered considerable discussion. As well as the main hall of the chapel, with its balcony along three sides, there was a large room on the ground floor, at the back, which Roddi decided was an ideal stable for Jerry, his horse. Above this room were two smaller rooms which became his bedroom and his living room-cum-office.

Over the next few weeks, Roddi put himself about among the villages of the Heath within half a day's journey from his base in Skinton. As he had told the old man on the bridge, he had pills and potions to sell for every ailment known to man. All very efficacious, he assured his customers. He quickly became a familiar figure throughout the area and people slowly came to accept and even trust this 'foreigner', probably because he never showed any inclination to con or swindle them. But this was merely a stopgap trade. Throughout those early weeks, he was preparing to launch his real line of business.

The large metal container with its firebox was, in fact, the main element of a distillation apparatus, a still, in other words. During the first weeks of his residency in Skinton, Roddi was building up a large stock of bootleg liquor. To this end, he had brought with him a supply of malted barley and potatoes plus flavourings to improve the potability of his products. The barley became "whiskey" while the potatoes yielded "vodka" of several different flavours. He intended to replenish these raw materials with locally grown produce. By an additional stroke of luck, the chapel was next door to an abandoned orchard, belonging to no one, and, it being Autumn, he was able to strip from it quantities of apples, pears and plums which, after fermentation, he distilled into more exotic spirits.

It was towards the end of October that Roddi Loach introduced his range of moonshine liquor to the people of the Heath. The only alcoholic drink available heretofore had been locally brewed beer of varying quality. A copious quantity of this brew was required by any individual wishing to become very happy or be rendered unconscious. Roddi's products achieved both these states much more quickly. The moonshine was a sensation, and it became clear that he would have to increase his output to meet demand and would therefore require help. Having let it be known that a couple of jobs were available, he was surprised by the very few candidates who came forward. The problem was that nearly everybody who could work was already working long hours to maintain a fairly basic level of existence.

Eventually, he took on two young people. Firstly, a lad of fifteen called "Sammo" who was, in local parlance, "touched," i.e., he had a volatile nature that shifted from docile to blazing aggression in seconds if something or someone upset him. As a result, no one was willing to risk giving him a job. Roddi saw something in the lad that others missed, especially his affinity for Roddi's horse, Jerry, and so gave him the task of looking after the horse as well as fetching and carrying jobs around the still.

His other new helper was a nineteen-year-old woman named Beth. She was unmarried, which was strange for someone of that age. The reason for this was the custom of "arranged" marriages among many families on the Heath. When she was twelve, Beth's parents had agreed to a marriage for her to Harry Spearman, also twelve, the son of a neighbouring farmer. The intention was that the couple would marry as soon as practical after they reached the age of sixteen. However, the nuptials were repeatedly postponed by Harry's miserly father, who could not persuade himself that the cost of supporting an additional family member could be justified and kept untruthfully pleading poverty whenever Beth's father tackled him about the matter. Beth had become fed up with all this procrastination and had decided to ease the burden on her parents by bringing in a wage herself. Roddi found her an apt pupil in learning the arts of distillation.

The success of his bootlegging business gave Roddi the idea of opening up a drinking establishment of his own. He screened off part of the chapel's balcony and furnished it with a random assortment of secondhand chairs and tables and a bar at one end. Beth served behind the bar. As he had hoped, this became a popular venue, particularly for the younger, male section of the Heath's population. Before long, Roddi had acquired the services of a musical group consisting of a fiddle, a guitar, drums, and a singer, who performed on weekends.

Roddi could never claim to be the most physically attractive of men, being on the short side with bandy legs and the feral look of a stoat, but he was articulate and amusing with an engaging manner. Also, beneath a hard-boiled outer shell, he had an essentially kind heart. He always seemed to have time to listen to his customers' moans about their lives. It wasn't long, therefore, before he had heard all about Beth's problems with her deferred marriage. It wasn't much longer before his sympathetic ear and kind words had beguiled the inexperienced young woman into believing that she had fallen in love with him. Being a still-youngish thirty-two-year-old, Roddi was not exactly reluctant to go along with this fantasy, and before the Christmas month had arrived, they were regularly taking their afternoon break together in Roddi's bed. To be fair to him, Roddi was genuinely fond of Beth and, in normal circumstances, might well have fallen in love and married her.

One such afternoon, lying comfortably exhausted beside each other, Beth said, 'You know, I half believed what people around here say about you wetlanders until I saw for myself.'

'What's that?' said Roddi.

'You've got webbed feet.' They both laughed.

'Well, now you've seen me in my natural state, you know we're no different to you Heath dwellers.'

'Oh, I wouldn't quite say that,' said Beth, 'there's the little matter of earrings and tattoos.'

'What's wrong with them? Where I come from, most men have earrings and tattoos.'

'Well, around here, any man wearing an earring – if he dared to – would be assumed to be a limp-wrister and get beaten up.'

'What the hell's a "limp-wrister"?'

'You know, one of those men who like other men instead of women.'

'Oh, I see. So everybody thought I was a "limp-wrister"', laughed Roddi. 'So why didn't they beat me up?'

'Because they could see you didn't exactly fit that bill and would probably give them more than they gave you if they tried it on.'

'Well, thank god for that. Anything else about me they don't like?' said Roddi.

'Your tattoos.'

'They're very common among my people.'

'Does everybody have them all over like you?'

'Depends on how much they like them or need them.'

'Why would they need them?'

'Well, some people just have one or two for decoration. Others have more to remember important things in their lives. For others, it's kind of identity markings, recognition signs for members of the same gang or religious group.'

'So, what are yours for?' asked Beth. 'You've got a hell of a lot of them and none of them can be seen except part of that one on your neck.'

'That means they're private. If I told you what they mean, you'd know everything about me. You'd own my soul.'

'Wow! Pretty important then.'

'Yup.'

Life continued much the same throughout the Autumn. Roddi's bar was a great success, drawing in drinkers from miles around. Too successful for that sector of the population, mainly female, who strongly disapproved of men squandering their substance in such a way. Resentment against Roddi began to be expressed more openly as Christmas approached. There was real concern underlying this resentment, for people knew that, in any society, since human beings first staggered into an upright position, there have always been more than a few only too willing and eager to fall back to the floor with the help of their old friend Al K. Holl. The outcome of this behaviour is almost always the reduction of the wastrel's nearest and dearest to poverty and penury. It was not surprising, therefore, that many people throughout the area wouldn't be sorry to see the back of Roddi.

A couple of weeks before Christmas, Beth's mother noticed that her usually active, cheerful daughter was sitting around moping, looking as if the world was coming to an end. Eventually, she could stand it no longer.

'Whatever's wrong, love?' she said. 'For the past couple of days you've been looking as if you'd lost a pound and found a penny.'

'I'm alright,' said Beth with so little conviction that her mother felt obliged to say,

'Well, if you're alright, I'd hate to see you when there was something wrong. Come on, love, tell me about it. When there's a problem, two heads are usually better than one for solving it.' Beth crumbled.

'It wouldn't make any difference if I had forty heads,' she wailed, tears streaming down her cheeks. 'It wouldn't solve this one.'

'Oh my God, whatever's happened?'

'I'm two months late. I'm pregnant.'

'What!' cried her mother. 'But you and Harry haven't.' She broke off in confusion. 'When did he do this?'

'He didn't. He's never been near me. He doesn't want to marry me, that's clear enough. And now he certainly won't. Nobody will.'

'So who's the lucky fella?'

'Him I work for. Roddi Loach.'

'He forced you, didn't he? He must have forced you.'

'No, Mum, he didn't. You might say I forced him. I certainly encouraged him. He's been so kind and understanding, I thought I loved him.'

Beth's father had the unenviable task of telling Harry's father the reason there would be no wedding now and that Harry had been released from the agreement. Harry's old man was delighted but managed to hide his pleasure behind a torrent of abuse of Beth and all her family.

Harry, himself, was upset but focused his ire on that 'bloody foreigner', Roddi Loach. He communicated this anger to his friends and relations and so to the world at large. A tide of anger began to gather against Roddi, swelling among those who believed his business operations were a scourge on society. It was not surprising, therefore, that plans soon began to be made to rid the Heath of this "web-footed, spawn of Satan, low-life, wetlander freak."

So it was, in late afternoon, a couple of days before Christmas, that a highly distressed Sammo burst into the Methodist chapel. Not the most articulate at the best of times, his story was difficult for Roddi to unravel.

'Roddi! Roddi! Don't want 'em to kill you,' he babbled. 'Kind to me, always was. Gev me a job. Coming tonight. Kill you an' burn this place down. Love Jerry. Don't want 'im 'urt either.'

'Whoa, Sammo,' said Roddi, putting his arm round the terrified boy's shoulders. 'Slow down. Who's coming? Why would somebody want to kill me?'

''Arry Spearman an' 'is mates an' a lot o' others who don't like you.'

'Harry Spearman? I hardly know him. Why would he come after me?'

''Cos o' Beth.'

'Beth? What's she got to do with it?' Sammo had calmed down and taken a deep breath before giving Roddi the bad news.

''Cos Beth was spoken for. For 'Arry. An' now she's 'avin your baby. 'E's goin' to kill
   you.'

'Hang on a minute, Sammo. I think you've got a bit mixed up. Who said Beth's having a baby? She's not said anything to me.'

'Beth told 'er mum. Said it was yours 'cos she an' 'Arry 'ave never done it.'

Roddi was afraid. He realised there was no way he could persuade the mob to call off its murderous plan. After all, he was guilty, wasn't he? He was sure Beth had no one else in tow who might be the father of her baby.

'Sammo,' he said, 'when are they coming?'

'Tonight. They're meeting up at 'Arry's place about seven o'clock. Goin' to burn everything. You as well. You got to go! Now! Get away! Fast as you can!' Sammo was almost incoherent with fear again.

'Right,' said Roddi. 'First things first. Sammo, I'm giving Jerry to you. I know you'll look after him. You know Albert Jenkins. Take Jerry to him and give Albert this for feed and shelter.' He took a thick wad of notes from his pocket and handed them to Sammo.

'And you keep on looking after Jerry like you have been doing for me.'

Sammo left the chapel on the run with Jerry. Roddi stuffed a backpack with essential items and left without a backward glance at the premises, which were burned down that night, along with any moonshine that remained after the place had been looted. The angry mob were doubly enraged by the disappointment of Roddi Loach escaping his just desserts.

Around sunset, it began to snow, lightly and fitfully at first, but soon an endless curtain of huge, wet, white flakes was sweeping across the twilit heathland. The east wind rose as if alarmed by this phenomenon, piling the snow into huge drifts wherever it could. The temperature plummeted below zero and remained within a degree or two either side of that frigid parameter for the following six weeks. During that time, bright, freezing days were interspersed with occasional snowstorms. All across the Heath, massive snowdrifts, many feet deep, blocked roads, and the villagers were forced to spend the Christmas period digging themselves out of their snowbound homes before they could tackle the blocked roads. There was little joy to be had at Christmas that year.

It was not until the middle of February that milder conditions arrived from the west, and the snow and ice covers began to melt. Slowly at first and then, with increasing rapidity, the white monster began to shrink, dwindling away to nothing, and the world was as if the snow had never been. It was then that a local shepherd, moving his flock to Spring pastures several miles west of Skinton, came upon the corpse of a man who must have fallen, during the first blizzard, into a disused stone pit and lain there, dead or dying, covered by several feet of snow.

The shepherd could see that these were not the remains of a local man by virtue of the gold ring in the left earlobe and the blue tattoo of something or other that could still be made out on the side of the decaying neck.

Les Dowse

TWO STORIES
By
Sheila Mayor

POTATO HARVEST

Here I am, 12 and a half years old in 1964. It's 7 am on a cold and frosty November morning. Tucked in my bed, candy-striped flannelette sheets, four woollen blankets, an eiderdown quilt, and a candlewick bedspread keeping me nice and warm. Two hot water bottles and flannelette pyjamas kept me in blissful slumber all night. I had been dreaming of those grown-up black sling-back shoes with kitten heels I was going to buy. A voice penetrated my dream world. 'AILEEN', my mum's voice telling me this was not the first time she had tried to get me up.

"Tattie picking", or "Tattie howking" was seasonal in October/November. Children would be given a school holiday to pick. This swelled the labour for the harvest and gave families much-needed money. By 1964, I don't remember us having "tattie" holidays from school; it was Saturday working only.

'It's time to get up, only half an hour until the lift comes.' Mum says.

Oh no, the day I dreaded had arrived. It's time to start easing into adulthood; get dressed and join in the potato harvest. Out of bed, dressing without washing, slipping woollen trousers over my pyjama bottoms, vest, 2 T-shirts, thick woollen polo neck jumper, finished off with thick socks Mum had knitted, tucked over my trousers. Down the stairs, quick teeth clean, a plate of porridge eaten in haste.

'Do you want two slices of toast for piece time?' asks Mum.

'Yes, please; I love bananas on cold toast.'

Not forgetting how very cold it was outdoors, I put on my navy blue, thick winter coat. I pulled my flappy ear hat firmly on my head, pushed my hands into red hand-knitted gloves and shoved my feet into black wellies.

Leaving the house and nice warm coal fire, mum and I walked a short distance to the end of the road. A noisy and smelly red tractor with an open farm bogey on the back turns into the road. "Massey Ferguson" in big letters on the bonnet, big wheels at the back and smaller wheels at the front, no cab to keep the driver covered.

'Come on then, let's be getting you lot on the bogey,' calls Davy Robertson, the tractor driver. He wears a flat cap at a jaunty angle, a cigarette hanging from his mouth.

'Two more pick-ups yit, ah've no got aw day.'

This could be the start of a worse day than I first thought. At the other stops, three more Mums, two girls and two boys made a full load aboard the bogey. Everyone is wrapped up against the cold, sitting on the floor, hanging on to the short sides, a bumpy ten-minute ride to the potato field.

'It's a rum day, the day, the cold would take the ears off you,' Mrs Balfour announced.

The hairs on her chin and upper lip gave the children something to stare at. Mums all wore the "Mums uniform" of winter coats, thick stockings, headscarves, and brown ankle boots with a zip-up front. The tractor driver whistled tunelessly on the bumpy ride, no care for the potato pickers hanging on in the back.

Once at the potato field, a very cold morning, frost on the ground, drills already harvested, brown tops on the potato shaws awaiting harvesting. The field looked huge to us, young starters.

'Right, we leave our piece bags here at the side of the field.' Mum said.

Mr Anderson, the driver of a big tractor with a covered cab and a fierce-looking metal machine fixed to the back, got out and darted towards the waiting women and children.

'Put yourselves where you want to be and we'll get the bits marked out.'

A man of few words, he bolted out the length of a designated adult "bit" and a "half bit" for the children, marking out with sticks. Davy Robertson drove another cart, loaded with creels made from latticed metal, dumping them alongside the "bits". Excitement mounting,

'Just do your best, you will soon pick it up, don't mistake stones for spuds,' said Mum.

Mr Anderson was back in his tractor, lining up the first row of potatoes to be dug. Seagulls were gathering all over the field, awaiting the start of the digging when worms the size of small snakes would be a feast time for them. As Mr Anderson came along the digger turning up potatoes, the earth had a lovely, sweet, clean smell. Time to bend over with the creel between your legs and start picking the potatoes as fast as possible. Filled creels were quickly put to the side, and another was grabbed, moving along the bit, trying not to look to see how much farther to the end. Mr Anderson had only one pace, very fast. No slacking or resting, the pace had to be kept up; everyone eventually settled into a rhythm. Davy Robertson drove a tractor with a side bogey alongside the pickers. His brother Peem and one of the older boys emptied the filled creels into the bogey and threw them back down, ready to be filled again.

'Put your back into it, nae slacking now, Mr Berwick's at the gate, watching to see who's no working, nae pay coming to the shirkers.'

These words of encouragement to the pickers from Davy and Peem.

Bit by bit, coats and jumpers were shed, and work soon heated up the workers. Putting them safely to the side, to be rescued and put back on later.

Piece time came after a couple of hours, and I was glad to collapse at the side of the field. Mum opened our piece bag and took out the cold toast and bananas. Tea was in a flask for Mum, and cold water in an empty lemonade bottle with a black screw stopper for me. Feeling better after a rest and some food, now came the time I was really dreading - when I needed the toilet. Mum and Lizzie's Mum held up their coats to make a shield so us girls could wee in private in the ditch. All too soon, it was back to picking, backs aching, trying not to think how long till dinnertime. Mr Anderson, by now the children's hated man, was back to his fast pace of digging,

Davy and Peem back to their teasing. Thinking of the money I would be paid and the shoes I coveted, I kept up the pace.

Dinnertime was a very welcome hour-long break. Everyone back to the side of the field, sitting together, unpacking sandwiches from the piece bags. I thought it funny that Lizzie Paxton's sandwiches were wrapped in a waxed bread wrapper; ours were wrapped in greaseproof paper. I felt posh. After cake and more water, there was time to rest. Lizzie and I walked up to the bank of trees to avoid the "coat toilet".

It was a long day, by afternoon piece time, I thought my back would break, and I nearly cried. Mum handed me a cake and a cup of tea.

'You are such a good wee worker, wait till I tell your dad, he will be so proud of you.'

The Mum's put the potatoes allowed for the day, a "boiling", into their now empty piece bags. Thinking of those wonderful shoes and telling Dad how hard I had worked kept me going to the end of that momentous day in my life. It was a new experience and one that, at that moment, I wasn't very keen on.

Mr Anderson's tractor fell silent, the cry went out "lowsin time", sitting down beside my last full creel of the day, relieved but happy. It had been good working with Mum. Back on the bumpy, bogey ride back to our street, I struggled off the bogey and hobbled home. When we got in, Mum took off her coat and started preparing dinner. Filling the bath with hot water and a handful of Mum's Lily of the Valley bath salts, I lowered myself into the delicious warm water, soothing my tired muscles. Closing my eyes, I could smell the lovely dinner Mum was preparing and thought of those black, sling-back, kitten-heeled shoes waiting for me in the shop.

Picture of potato harvesting of the era - credit Facebook.

Sheila Mayor

A GREAT CALAMITY

Snow had been around for weeks, the ground was frozen, and the air was crisp and clear. Children had hours of fun making slides and sledging in the fields. With only four weeks to Christmas Day 1962, Tommy Purdy was hoping for a train set from Santa. He saw the box in a toy shop in Edinburgh when shopping with his Granny. A picture of a model engine, red and shiny, two carriages and lengths of track were in the set. He planned to make papier-mâché tunnels and trackside banking. He asked Mr Donaldson, their next-door neighbour, to save his old newspapers for him, and his Mum made up the flour-and-water paste for him. He talked about that train set at least once a day, since he wrote a letter to Santa. He could only dream of unwrapping that shiny, red train set on Christmas Day.

Tommy ran out of school at 3.30 pm, eager to get home. It was Beano comic day; it was his turn to read it first before his sister Rona. Pulling his long grey trousers up by the red and black snake belt, Fair Isle knitted jumper rumpled up under his black woollen jacket, Tommy pulled on the balaclava his Granny had knitted for him. He jumped over a low wire fence into the small field next to the school — a shortcut home, cutting cut a long path. It was precarious to run at Tommy's speed on the slippery grass, but his boots had a good sole on them, great for a quick dart home. Tommy was ten, a wiry, small boy for his age, with fair hair cut in a short back-and-sides style. He was a happy-natured boy who always ran errands for his Mum and neighbours without complaining. His granny called him 'Billy Whiz' as he ran whenever he could.

Soon, he was over the last fence, making his way along the back gardens of the prefabs, running up a path to the left of the boundary fences, to the main road. The prefab housing scheme sat on either side of Glebe Road, a main road. Grey single-story houses with corrugated iron roofs. Tommy lived in one with his mum, dad and sister. The prefab had a solid, brown wooden front door with one window on one side and two on the other. A slightly sloping metal roof with a chimney flue poking out the top. A small, low-fenced front garden faced the main road. The prefabs were built as emergency housing in the town of Gilbertown, near Edinburgh, just after the Second World War.

Tommy stopped outside his gate. The slide he and his playmates had made on the pavement yesterday had melted; a mum had been out and poured salt on it. All fun is gone until the next snowstorm. Tommy opened the front door, kicked off his boots and pulled off his balaclava as he stepped into the lobby.

'Tommy, keep your coat on, you'll run a message for me, ' shouted his Mum from the kitchen. Tommy's sister made a face at him, sitting warm and cosy at the table. Sorting through her paper 'scraps', ready to create a new design in her scrapbook. The Beano would have to wait until after tea. Tommy's boots and balaclava went back on.

'Go to the grocers for a bag of broken biscuits, a slab of butter and the chemist for a blade for your dad's razor. Mind to ask for the 7 O'clock one, his mum said, giving Tommy two £2 notes folded up. Tommy rolled up the shopping bag his Mum had given him and popped it under his arm.

Tommy liked running errands. Across the road from his house, he waved to Mr Toner, the coal man, as he delivered bags of coal to the prefab opposite. A majestic Clydesdale horse, with a coloured coat and a white blaze down its nose and white legs, pulls the coal cart. Coal bags were stacked, ready to be lifted. Mr Toner's command to the horse as he moves on from house to house is, "giddy along there, Mister Buchanan." Tommy has no idea why the horse has a man's name.

He slowed his usual running pace, taking his time down the hill to the shops. The slush was more slippery than the ice, and the hill was steep.

Into the chemist's first, single blade in its wax wrapper purchased and put safely in his trouser pocket. Tommy enjoyed feeling grown up by handling a sharp, safely wrapped blade. The grocer's shop was next door, and sixpence worth of broken biscuits from Mr Mitchell would last the family a few days.

'Now, young Tommy, this thaw has put paid to your slides for a while. The grannies will be safe from going arse upwards. Ha! Ha!'

Mr Mitchell always had a friendly word for Tommy.

Tommy was smirking at the grocer, saying 'arse' when a great commotion of shouts and noise made them both turn to look out of the door. Mr Mitchell pulled him away from the front of the shop.

'Jings, get behind the counter, young Tommy.'

Mister Buchanan was slipping and sliding down the hill, the coal cart swaying behind him, bags fell off, and lumps of coal flew everywhere. Mr Toner stood at the top of the hill with his hands on his head, not believing what was happening to his beloved Mister Buchanan. Crouched down behind the counter, Tommy and Mr Mitchell could only hold their breath and listen to the noise of crashing like a bomb exploding. They slowly got up and looked over the counter to see glass and wood scattered across the road outside. The horse had crashed straight into the window of the chemist's shop. An eerie silence fell. Mister Buchanan was lying on his side, not moving. Mr Gillespie, the chemist, pushed himself out of the smashed shop door. Unhurt but dazed, he looked down at the horse as Mr Toner arrived. Both men could only look at the poor horses' injuries in disbelief; nothing could be done, as it was fatally injured.

Tommy's mum was soon on the scene, holding Tommy tight to her, crying with relief.

'Thank goodness you went to the chemist first. '

The memory of the mayhem and bloodshed would stay with Tommy for the rest of his life.

The great calamity was never forgotten, and the story was passed on to other generations over the years.

In 2002, Mike McAllister, an American through and through (but extremely proud of his Scottish heritage), visited the area where his parents grew up. A scriptwriter, whose business with a film company in Edinburgh had gone well. By now, he had a couple of days off before his flight back to America, in time for Thanksgiving.

Mike was looking forward to seeing Gilberstown, eager to walk the same streets his parents once did and hoped to feel closer to the lives they left behind before emigrating to the States.

Approaching the town, Mike noticed a recent good fall of snow. The side of the road and pavements had a good build-up of slush. Slowing his speed, he passed a school to his left, and a caretaker was unlocking black metal gates. Mike pulled up the car; this must be the school his parents had attended. Next to the school is the large field his dad told him about, where the children would run through as a shortcut home. He got out of his car to take a photo; he had promised his parents to get views of the area where they grew up.

Crossing over the road to the park opposite the school to take the shot, a cold mist filtered ghost-like through the sycamore trees lining the road. Over a low grey stone wall bordering the park, swings and slides sat silently. A lady dressed in bright blue Lycra caught his eye, making use of the outdoor gym equipment. Mike smiled at her dedication on such a cold morning. He imagined children playing and families enjoying themselves on sunny days; his parents told him of happy days spent in the park growing up. He can recall them reminiscing about snowball fights and building snowmen; in those days, the snow would lie for weeks, and making slides was a favourite form of entertainment.

Shivering with cold, Mike got back in the car. Setting off again, his sat nav had a woman's voice. Her English accent made him smile.

She said, 'In 50 metres, turn left into Glebe Road.'

Turning into Glebe Road, the view looked nothing like the photos his parents had shown him of the area in the 1960s. No prefabs with big gardens now. Blocks of houses, close together, brown bricks with russet roof tiles, looking as if they are standing to attention. So different from his hometown in Connecticut.

Pulling the car into a layby, Mike hoped he was near his parents' prefab housing. He takes his camera out of its bag, ready to take more photos. A lady, holding a dark brown spaniel on a lead, passed him, smiling, she greeted him with a 'good morning'. Mike returned the lady's greeting, so different from his home neighbourhood, where people rarely walk anywhere.

Mike stood still, taking photos, imagining how people lived back in his parents' day. Life would have been different for families then, and it would have been a great place for children to grow up. His parents have wonderful childhood memories of the games they played in the street.

He strolled down the hill to the row of shops at the bottom; they face up the hill from Clunie Way. A shop front stands out. Black-and-white frontage: a large window sits on either side of a black-painted door. A large glass globe hangs above the door with the word 'Chemist'. The chemist's name is written in black across the top of the shop front. The shop looked old-fashioned compared to the others. Mike took a photo of the shop and then wandered inside.

'Good morning to you,' Mike greeted the man behind the counter. 'I just love your storefront.'

The pharmacist, who appeared to be around fifty years old with short grey hair and a round, smiling face, greeted Mike.

'Good morning to you, sir. Glad you like it; can I help you?'

'I could use some antacids, whatever you recommend, I clean forgot to pack mine before I left the States. '

'Have a look at the shelf behind you; there's quite a selection.'

Mike chose a pack and took them to the counter.

'I'm in the neighbourhood visiting where my parents grew up, they told me all about their years here and what it was like. Stories of how the neighbours looked out for each other; kids played safely in the street. They emigrated to Connecticut in the early 1970s. Looking down the hill, it reminded me of a tale my parents told me. It always fascinates me, it's about a horse pulling a coal cart that bolted down the hill in icy weather, crashing into a shop. A sad story,' said Mike.

'Well, Sir, I can tell you that the story is true and lives with me every day.'

The chemist looked emotional as he took a deep breath and continued his tale.

'I was a wee boy out getting messages for my mum, I had just left this chemist shop and was in the grocers next door.' The grocer, Mr Mitchell, pulled us both behind the counter when he saw the horse and cart careering down the hill. No idea where it would crash into. She got down here as fast as she could to look for me. You see, she had sent me to the chemist and could see the poor horse had crashed straight through the chemist's window. When I appeared from the grocer's door, she grabbed hold of me and nearly broke my ribs; she held me so tight. She was in shock for days after. When I qualified as a pharmacist, I bought this shop when it came on the market years ago. I decided to keep the frontage as it was after being rebuilt and renamed it 'Buchanan's' in memory of the horse.'

'What a story,' Mike is spellbound. 'Will you let me take a photo of you and your store?'

'Certainly, I would be delighted. I hope you show it to your parents; they will recognise the shop, I'm sure.'

'They surely will, tell me your name; they may remember your folks.'

'Thomas Purdy, tell them I lived at number 58 Glebe Road with my parents and sister Rona'.

'Sure will, it's a pleasure to speak with you, Thomas, and hear your story.'

'Well, I'll be darned,' thought Mike to himself as he left the shop.

'Wait till I tell the folks I met the survivor of the bolting horse.'

Sheila Mayor

A POEM AND A STORY
By
Malcolm Nez

THE CYCLISTS VILLANELLE

Composed whilst walking and cycling the Leicestershire Round, Summer 2025.

The summer lanes of quiet English counties
Are holidays themselves for cycling round
To quaint old villages and hostelries.

So much is empty pastoral counties.
Where floral fragranced rural acres found -
Hedgerows to forage sloes and blackberries.

The hedgerow crab and ripening orchard trees.
Their windfalls lie around upon the ground,
Near quaint old villages and hostelries.

The summer fields of corn or other bounties,
Of grazing for the beasts and game around,
Fill butcher's, poulterer's, larder or granaries.

Save for the birds and summer's buzzing bees,
Along the green lane scarce of *any* sound,
The quietude — does nurse the ragged senses.

Then screeching downhill 'twixt the weather-vaned spires;
Legs and pedals blur and whirr around.
Announcing the cyclist to the local clergy,
Police and quaint old village hostelries.

Malcolm Nez

IN A SPIN

As father and daughter, we stayed with friends. Sitting in the evening, finding less and less to say, my attention turned to the local paper. In rural Scotland, the area covered was large.

'Where is Ballykintyre?' I asked.

'Oh,' Joyce answered, 'It isn't far. Why do you ask?'

So, I answered. 'It says here that there is a fête followed by a ceilidh tomorrow. Do you think Lizzie and I could get there?'

The subject was discussed. It seemed we could drive there in less than 30 minutes, that the roads were very narrow, and that we should take them slowly. People have spun off the road in a few places, so caution was advised. Winter wet leaves would be an ever-present danger. It was agreed that we would leave late morning and have our lunch at the fête, returning after the ceilidh.

The Scottish west coast weather is well known for rain: it rains to some extent most days. Today was no exception, teeming down when we rose from our beds but easing as the morning progressed.

Breakfast was really lovely with lots of cereal, toast, tea or coffee and restful, meaningless conversation. Then, at 11 AM, we found ourselves too relaxed to move. We looked at each other and realised it was now or never. Lizzie and I made a pile of waterproofs, woollens, walking boots, wellington boots, hats, gloves, etc. I brought the car round, we packed and set off as torn grey clouds showed blue here and there.

I was feeling rather buoyant and offered 'The clouds have lifted, which augurs well. We can expect to have a lovely day.'

I was warned. 'Dad, don't watch the clouds or the skies. This is a dangerous road - so look at it!'

'Right you are,' I agreed.

All was going well until we rounded a corner with a broad

patch of wet leaves. I just touched the brakes momentarily, and the car was travelling slowly, sideways, towards a barrier. I steered into the skid, frightened of the brakes, but using them all the same, the wheels gripped on shreds of tarmac between skeins of mud and leaves, and we stopped or were stopped. I swallowed hard, wound the window down and peered out to see about six inches of clear space between the car and the barrier.

'It's alright,' I said, 'we haven't hit anything.'

'Well, that was lucky, Dad,' said Lizzie with some relief.

'So, what did I do wrong?' I asked.

'Probably nothing, Dad. It's a dangerous road.'

The spin had been disorienting. We nearly set off in the direction from which we had just come until Lizzie told me, rather impatiently, to make a 3-point turn to continue in the original direction.

'Yes, you're quite right,' I accepted and made the necessary manoeuvre.

The road widened, was clear of leaves, and all was going well until a shout in my ear alerted me.

'Slow down! We're approaching adverse camber.'

'Have I missed the sign?' I asked.

'No! Just look at the road and the corner,' was the answer.

I was braking and steering, never a good combination, changing gear for an uphill section and running out of road — again. By now, I was perspiring from every pore and gripping the perspiration-coated wheel. This was becoming a white-knuckle ride. We were in mid-S bend.

We got around on two wheels and a prayer. Heavens, this was frightening. As the car settled, we hit leaves again, but slowly and safely. Controlling myself at this point was as much a challenge as controlling the vehicle. So far, we hadn't encountered oncoming traffic, and my nerves were shaking me like barley stalks in a gale.

'Lizzie,' I said, 'this is terribly dangerous.'

No answer, not at first. Then, when we reached a straight section, she replied,

'Yes, Dad, I have noticed. We can't take anything for granted. Skid hazards, leaves, water, mud, etc., animals, especially livestock, oncoming traffic, and potholes. It's all there for us, and combinations of these, too. The only solution is to drive slowly.'

I slowed to walking pace where I was unsure, but increased to 20mph along straight sections. In this fashion, we made it to Ballykintyre. I parked and could not get to the toilets and tea tent fast enough. We found a bench and gathered our wits. I explained to Lizzie that there was a red flag in the boot, which I thought we might need later on.

'I'm going for a look round, Dad.'

Lizzie announced her intentions, leaving me to my thoughts and a few moments of much-needed mindfulness. It might have looked odd, but I wasn't bothered what other people thought, and of course, this is Scotland, where people are too mannerly to say, well, at any rate, *rural* Scotland is like that.

My attention returned to the sky, which was holding up. 'Dad, the fell race is due to start right over there, ' called out Lizzie.

They go up this side of the wall, over the knoll, turn away from us for a while, but then return. Down the far side with a hair-raising descent.'

'What!' I replied. 'That's a death trap.'

'I'd prefer it to your driving,' she said with a cheeky grin.

I pointed out that perhaps I would too. No need to make an issue of it, I thought, you'll only lose.

The starting pistol fired, and off they went. A bunch became a string, and a string became several well-spaced, smaller bunches before the leaders ran over the knoll. It's a good spectator sport, we agreed, and the last runners trailed out of sight.

'When does the ceilidh start?' I asked.

'Not until 5 PM.....Well, we can get an hour or two dancing before we must leave. So, let's consider any other attractions between now and then. They've got sheep shearing and penning. They've got rabbits and fowl. They've even got remotely controlled model helicopters,' Lizzie replied.

'Aye, they have,' said a voice from behind us.

As we turned to face the speaker, he continued, 'but it's a demonstration, you dinna get to fly them yerselves.'

'Understood.' I said. The voice continued.

'They have video cameras and they're projecting the full race on a big screen over there.'

So they are I realised and thanked the man.

Lizzie and I went to see, just as many others drifted along. Standing before the screen, it was obvious that the going was rough for the runners. Some fell, many were plastered in mud. As they ran over rocks and turf, through streams, over boulders and around markers, the lead changed repeatedly. No one stood out as a likely winner.

In fact, Lizzie observed, 'No one is guaranteed to finish.'

The race marshals were helping runners who had fallen to their feet and checking them for injuries.

The rain fell gently but persistently, and I remembered my father telling me that in weather like this, the electricity in the overhead cables can jump 13 feet. Mmm. I thought. They have pylons up there; surely the helicopter pilots know what they are doing, and surely the race organisers do too. They wouldn't have exposed the runners to risk, would they? As we look at the channel between two cliff faces, a sudden flash of blue and green appears. Sudden — then suddenly gone, and I shuddered.

'Aagh!' I gasped, 'Did you see that?'

Turquoise, sky blue, emerald green, royal blue in quick succession. An uninterrupted sequence, continuous colour. Flashes that, from a distance, made me fearful.

'Were there electrocuted runners up there. Should I speak to the organisers?' I must have spoken my thoughts aloud.

'No,' said Lizzie, 'it's not that difficult. The colours are runners' vests. There will be red and yellow soon enough,'

Indeed, there was; by this time, the cameras had zoomed in. Just for a few seconds, I was shaken; my nervous electricity, albeit at a lower voltage, had shocked me more than the runners were shocked.

'I might need a sit-down,' I said.

'Breathe deeply and keep watching,' Lizzie commented.

Those running towards us were at the front and had precipitous paths down. Only proper mountain fell racing footwear would see them safe, and those towards the back would be confronted by a sea of mud concealing jagged rock here and there.

'Look, Dad, they're approaching the way down.'

This was about 20 minutes into an expected 30-minute race. Tension was mounting. I could have run a book, offered odds, and taken wagers. Then I realised I had no idea about the law and who the faster runners were. Another daft idea bites the dust and rightly so.

And now the runners emerge from the hinterland into view. Each chooses their preferred path from several running in parallel, but over different terrain. They pour down as the rain once more. The mud splatter camouflages the faces reddened by wind-driven rain. They show anguish, breathlessness and gritty determination. Knees pumping, nose to the front, careering downhill, right shoulder pointing ahead, then switching to the left.

The dark blue vest is ahead—oh, heavens, he's fallen or slipped or been tripped, and now he's back up but several places behind. Purple vest is in the lead with a bloodied arm, but now yellow overtakes, and there's pushing and shoving, so both tumble, return to their feet, and struggle to gain the best ground. Red vest is now leading, leaps over footstool-sized rocks, turns in the air to face left, lands with left foot uphill, skids, slides and twists and turns to the right, continually switching. A fascinating display of speed and balance.

But the green vest is now gaining - a blur of busy feet on probably the better path, but it's a path that joins with and diverges from others.

Green and red are approaching a pinch point neck-and-neck. Green launches into the air to drop ahead of red, but red skates on the rain-drenched, gravelly scree, careering out of control to pass green. One is going to land on the other, but didn't; the scree petered out, red slowed, and green stayed ahead. The spectator's excitement grows with the expectancy of predicting the outcome. Although the pink vest has passed blue and yellow, it makes a determined bid for the lead. Pink, however, is running a slower path, with too many rocky outcrops.

Green wins, red second, pink third, then various shades of blue, orange, and, from earlier, purple, which comes in about tenth with many stragglers, where I would have been in years gone by. We are thoroughly impressed by their performance and the spectacle. Applause continues for several minutes. Prizes are awarded, and slowly the spectators ebb away as the excitement dissipates.

Lizzie and I go to look at the helicopters, but her attention is drawn to some sheep corralling. It involves removing barriers from a trailer, winding them out to form a pen, filling it with sheep, then reversing the process on the referee's signal. All against the clock.

'Are you interested?' I ask.

'Yes, of course I'm joining Team Green,' says Lizzie.

There are two teams, team orange and team green.

My interest in the helicopters is the engine. The aircraft themselves would scarcely fit in the boot of a car. For engines, it turns out they use gas turbines of nearly 1 litre. Roughly the size of a small kettle. The diameter is about half the length. They make a lovely, containing but disconcerting scream as they wind up to full power. I am captivated; I want one; I've no use for one —but is that really relevant? Well, after exhausting all my questions, which were adroitly answered, I turned my attention to Lizzie and her new sport.

The official has started them, and being a minute or two into the race, they are winching out the fence barriers, connecting them and somehow bodies are doubling around the equipment, each performing a task like seasoned professionals. Maybe one or two have farm connections, maybe not —but it is highly efficient. Progress is rapid. I look at team orange and estimate how much progress they have made, then do the same for team green. By the time I look at orange again, they have flown ahead. Back to team green, and they are gaining. It isn't possible to compare one with the other — well, for me, it isn't. Possibly the officials can tell at a glance, but change is so rapid. Now they are moving sheep. Team orange is the first, but they haven't secured their fences, and the sheep are out as fast as they are in. All hands to gather and redirect. Someone fixes things whilst team green has secure fences and sheep flowing efficiently. Quite rapid progress.

The judges give the nod to both teams almost simultaneously. The activity starts again. Sheep out into the pen from whence they came - they seem to be enjoying it, and perhaps it is a game for them as well. A few sheep nuts might be involved, although I can't see properly. They then disconnect the hurdles, dismantle the pen and winch the whole back onto the trailer. Team Green was slick. They had learned more from the first half of the operation and had become more proficient. By a short fleece, Team Green wins.

After a good round of applause, Lizzie and I head for refreshment. It's gone 4 PM, and as we queue, we talk about the day so far. Refreshing weather, good organisation, lots of interest, lots more to come, worthwhile making the effort, ready for a rest. 'Yes. Two teas please and two scones with crowdie and raspberry jam.' The lady served us, and we carried our purchases away.

We had to share a table, and, after sitting for an hour, we sagged back in our chairs. After all, it had been near-constant excitement. The other occupants of the table were discussing the band that was to play the ceilidh music. Some were already in the showground. The fiddler is Shetland-trained. There's a clarsach and an electric bass, too. Other instruments to follow. We also heard there is a bar. Lizzie gave me a firm, stern look. I nodded in agreement. Note to self – one drink, two at the most, to be consumed before the bulk of the dancing and at least an hour before driving back. Dancing will burn up the alcohol. Lizzie reminded me that the licensing laws have changed; even a half pint of beer can cause you to fail the breath test.

We finished our refreshments by which time it was approaching 5 PM. We now wandered around, looking at the livestock and the judging — rabbits and fowl, mostly, cattle and sheep. A display of falconry settled the audience. Quietly, we chatted about our holiday so far — no bad words to say; everything has been a good experience, and there are no fears for tomorrow. Much to look forward to.

With an alcoholic drink in hand, I watched as the band set up. Lizzie just had fruit juice. Mostly, I would drink the same as her, but this was a special day, a day that had thrilled me. My vigorous exercise for the day would be a dance, nothing too demanding. One thing I look forward to is asking a lady to dance. It remains a thrill, even at my age.

And the music began. A country air and a few fiddle tunes to get us warmed up — enjoyable. Feet tapping, hands clapping, people arriving, drawn in by the sound. Then they announced they would play some dance tunes if anyone wished to dance. Now I had better describe things.

I explained that it had been raining on and off throughout the day, so the ground was wet. As it was raining and generally muddy, I was wearing Wellington boots, which would be alright, I supposed. Appropriate for the weather but possibly not for the activity — you can't have everything, can you? I was unsure whether boots would provide too much grip and not enough slip-slide, or vice versa, giving too much slip-slide.

The first dances were gentle and slow. A lady with light brown hair and a knee-length dress danced a Schottische solo, which was delightful. Her hair and dress floated so easily that she got air beneath them and retained it whilst spinning and leaping. Most people were rather pleased to watch others clap along to the rhythm, with some enthusiasm. The chatter at the bar dropped to a whisper. That solo dance piqued our interest. The ceilidh was underway, and we took to the floor.

We commenced with the "Water of Leith", danced to a lovely Strathspey. "Dashing White Sergeants" followed, which was not quite as testing as it sounds, although we had quickened pulse and breath just the same. Really enjoyable; country dancing of all types relies on teamwork, with participants guiding each other through the steps we'd been shown but had partly forgotten. We sat for a few minutes while someone arranged some coloured disco lighting here and there. These coloured lights were equipped with flashes that somehow picked up the music's beat.

Back on our feet again, we were prepared for something a little more adventurous. It was such a delight to ask the lady in the knee-length dress whether she would care to dance, and an even greater delight when she accepted. Standing together, awaiting the opening bars, I realised the lady was quite petite, and, before we could exchange names, we were away. Two dances, "The Bon Viveur" and "The Duke of Perth," followed, and a few more couples appeared on the dance floor. The general mood was one of enthusiasm; all too often, people sit on the edges of the room but do not partake in the dancing. Today was different. The band were beginning to win. The dances went smoothly, well, more or less. Nothing discouraging anyway.

A few more dances followed at a faster pace still. I was really enjoying myself. The lights flashing, interspersed with snatches of darkness, where we had to use our spatial awareness, was challenging but fun. Smiles all around, mostly, but punctuated with blank stares of concentration. We needed our wits about us.

In this way, the pace quickened, and the senses were dominated by vivid colour, spinning, pulse, music and breathlessness. With the quickening pace came more involved dance figures. By this time, the petite lady in the knee-length dress and I had introduced ourselves. She was Jeannie, and I was Malcolm. I went back to Jeannie and asked her again to dance. Jeannie accepted. Finally, they had us fast and furiously "Stripping The Willow."

"Strip the Willow" wearing waterproofs and wellies. Try saying that quickly. Tongue twisters are a lovely way of learning to laugh at our mistakes and our inability to control things at speed. Speaking of which, I had coped with the rhythms and tempo up to now, with the odd rest quite naturally. So far, so good. Jeannie had got the measure of my weight and height as she spun me in a hold.

I said to my dancing partner, 'Not quite so energetic, Jeannie, it's not a martial art.'

Well, she might have heard, or she might not, but with all the casting off, leading to the first corners, forming a star, reversing, leading up, circle round 2, 3, now anticlockwise, etc. It all became something of a blur for me. The lights were flashing, and as Jeannie spun me round, I began to lose touch with reality. I am not a sufficiently good dancer to spot my gaze whilst spinning. Moreover, when the lights changed and my attempted spot switched off, flashed or moved, I lost my target and then my footing.

Too many people on the dance floor was one of the problems. As my wellies lost traction, I slipped and slid, careering into spinning couples. We all seemed to go down somewhere between dominoes and Jenga. Each of us is beneath someone yet sprawled over someone else. What a knot that was to untie. And yet, not a dry eye in the house. So much laughter. The band stopped; the disco lighting changed to regular white. By the time we had stopped laughing and the tangle was untangled, we all realised that, in reality, the day's entertainment was over. I seconded a proposal of thanks to the organisers, and we applauded for several minutes.

The walk to the car park was rather quiet, a few moments to gather one's thoughts and recover a little from the day's excitement.

'Dad, you still haven't explained the red flag,' Lizzie looked quizzical.

'Well, I said I'd like you to carry it.'

After a short pause, she said, and very emphatically said, 'Oh! No. I don't think so.'

'It's safer on the way back,' we were advised.

'You'll no need the lassie with the flag walking ahead. Just keep yer speed down.'

Safer? Surely not by much, I thought.

We set off in high spirits but were continually checking our enthusiasm. Our heightened concentration seemed to work. I have always driven more slowly after dark, and headlights are very useful warnings of oncoming traffic. Using all these advantages got us home safely.

Joyce and Dennis were waiting for us. With little or nothing on the telly, they mashed some tea, found some scones, and we swapped highlights of our day for theirs. What caused the greatest intrigue was who Jeannie was. They considered the different families in the district, and being a combination of nurse and builder, they knew a great many people, yet without success. Jeannie was, and remains, a mystery.

Then I recounted the incident while dancing "Stripping the Willow."

'Oh! That is easily explained,' and Joyce revealed that the petite women spin you around the fastest.

'How so?' I asked.

'Don't know — but they do,' answered Joyce.

Malcolm Nez

A STORY

By
Tony O'Dwyer

A BRUSH WITH MARILYN
Fantasy Screenplay

The studio was a cage. The lion of British art paced to and fro. Lucian smote his easel with a big brush. The smack resonated around the crumbling room.

'Three hours late!' he barked. 'Three hours late!'

'I'll paint her arse with iodine when she gets here for the bruising. I can't stand being stood up by models. Time is millions, even if it is by Marilyn. She, above all, should know a serious artist cannot be kept waiting,' he said to himself irritably.

'I'll paint her arse with iodine over and over again.'

'Marilyn's here,' called his assistant from below. Lucian's talking to himself tails off only to give way to butterflies in his stomach. He looks at the studio door in nervous anticipation.

After what seems an eternity, a figure glides into the work area. A figure that is at once small and unassuming. A figure that has made some effort to be anonymous, with coat epaulettes turned up, sunglasses as big as saucers. Jeans and short boots – only a fluff of blonde hair gave a clue to her identity. She has arrived as Norma Jean Baker. As she removed her glasses, the celebrity Marilyn emerged immediately radiant.

A light in the drab studio-one, that would dazzle, disarm, bewitch and disturb any red-blooded male in the vicinity. The greatest living painter of the human figure, the veteran of countless nude portraits, was no exception. He was surprised to find himself nervous, twitching, and smiling helplessly.

'Well, Hello, Mr Freud. It's such a privilege to be in your studio,' she whispered audibly.

'You are somewhat late, but a thousand welcomes,' Lucian croaked drily

'Oh, I am sorry, Mr Freud, but I had to get my beauty sleep. Filming was endlessly gruelling. Larry is so meticulous, such a pain in the butt. I've had to psyche myself up to do this. You don't want to paint me as a drooping figure with bags under my eyes now, do you?' Marilyn said, muttering, her eyelashes.

'That's just how I want to paint. And please call me Lucian. And please, could we start? I've got debts as long as my brush and I need to complete this work before the enforcers come knocking at me door.'

'I can see you've got a big brush,' said Marilyn, breathlessly eyeing him up and down. 'You must have a lot of debt.'

The character and condition of the studio caught her attention —bare boards, a slimy sink, a battered sofa, a dirty floor— all presided over by a bulb without a shade. Dirty paint pots held worn brushes. The smell of oil paint pervaded everything.

'What a dump,' Marilyn exclaimed.

The star shivered.

'I don't want to touch anything.'

'Please go behind the screen, Mariyln. You can remove your garments there. You're professional; you've done all this before for photographers. This time it is art,' is Freud's tetchy response, directing her with his brush.

Marilyn went behind the Chinese lacquered screen, not noticing a strategically placed mirror on the other wall. As she disrobed — glasses, scarves, coat, blouse, jeans, boots, and nickers — the moving image in the mirror was that of a beautiful burlesque performer. A blonde angel emerging from the grey surroundings. A picture of peachy, pearlescent pulchritude. A radiant sculpture of flesh. A modern visual echo of the old masters -Rubens, Titian, Boucher.

The full Marilyn emerged. Her nudity enhanced her beauty. The less garments she wore, the more beauty she exuded. Lucian had a model from heaven, far from the earth of his usual sitters. His head hit with a tsunami of feelings, memories and perceptions; long ago, love at first sight, a remembrance of callow youth, darkened cinemas, a hurried comparison of former lovers, the problems of rendering flesh tones. All converged to perplex the modern master on his latest commission. A sudden, rare shaft of sunlight. Illuminates her pubic hair, turning it to gold against the milky purple of her shaded stomach.

The vision demolishes the last barricade of his anger.

'Do you want me to sit or lie on the couch, Lucian?' Marilyn asks.

'Please lie on it. Make yourself as comfortable as possible. Had you been a professional art model, I would want a more strenuous pose. Here I would like something more languid, more sensuous. Park your bottom on the sofa. Put your head to one side....Yes, that's it, put your feet there.... just there.'

She drapes herself onto the old, inhospitable sofa.

'How about this pose? I think I'm as comfortable as I'll ever be.'

'I am sure you are,' smiles Lucian.

'Was Sigmund Freud a relation, Lucian?'

An unexpected question in the circumstances.

'Yes, he was my grandfather,' Lucian replies, holding the brush.

'Gee, fancy having Sigmund Freud as a grandfather!'

'My grandfather put the human mind in its reality. I put the human body in its reality – not the glamourised version of the contemporary era......Can we get on with this?' We are running late.' Lucian almost stammers as he goes on.

Marilyn is somewhat wide-eyed by this little lecture but says nothing and stares ahead, preparing to be a new fleshy masterpiece from the drabness of Kensington.

'Ouch,' shouts Marilyn. 'There's a spring sticking in my ass!'

'Then find another spot to park your ass, and could you move your left leg. I need to paint more of your middle part.'

'I need to paint more of your middle part,' mimics Marilyn in an English accent and continues in American.

'I don't want my middle parts flashed all over London.'

'It's not a Lucian Freud if there is no middle part,' he responds.

'It's not a Marilyn if there is a middle part,' she snaps.

'It's a painting, not a diagram for a medical dictionary.'

The artist goes into a silent sulk–the greats are being thwarted again. His hand holding the brush at his side, his mouth down, keeping in an unbearable silence before Marilyn moves her leg.

'That will have to do,' he snorts as he sees up to the canvas.

Marilyn seems more beautiful as she gazes from the couch - a sad, chastened young woman, wistful perhaps of the onrush of middle age.

Lucian attacked the canvas with the big brush. He proceeds — by slashing, slapping, staring... stabbing, sighing, staring... swearing, wiping, staring... snarling, rubbing, staring... sniffing, stamping, staring... smudging, skimming staring, caking, raking staring... staining, teeth baring staring.

The brown skid marks give way to patches of colour. The tones of flesh are layered onto the studio greys as a figure and its surrounds appear on the canvas. The master changed to smaller flat brushes as he scooped up the knife-blended paint. As much as he tried, his usual well-observed silver flesh tones would not appear. He wanted to paint Norma Jean, but an unfinished Marilyn was on the board. Splendid on the couch, a star rising above circumstance, sunlight in the London gloom.

The figure leapt off the canvas, transfixing the viewer. The other pictures in the studio paled in comparison. Paint was turned into flesh. Marilyn had arrived, her face ghostly in the earth colours.

The suggestion was more powerful than the obvious.

She twitched under his bird of prey scrutiny.

'You'll know me when you see me again,' she chirped.

'What do you think of when you're painting, Lucian?'

The question came with a slightly provocative movement of the hip, which elicited a tolerant sigh from the artist, who eventually said:

'Going to the pub in Soho and having a drink with Francis Bacon.'

'Wow, Francis Bacon,' exclaims his sitter, gushing. 'David Sylvester thinks he's the world's greatest artist.'

'Balderdash,' spits Lucian, 'I'll wring his scrawny neck. I'll put dog muck on his doorstep......I'll.. I'll ...He really is a printed toad!'

Marilyn ran her eye over the studio and around the artist, keeping herself from moving.

The large room with its grubby sink, copper taps green with mould, the bare boards floor, bare brickwork, spidery plants, coloured sofa, window blinds, down an old pair of boots, paint-splattered cloths slung from the walls, a battered, floral-patterned armchair.

Marilyn tried to chat again.

'What do you do when you're not painting, Lucian? Don't you have hobbies?'

'I don't have hobbies, I have passions. It's a passion for gambling that's driving me to do this commission. I owe some people a lot of money. If I don't pay, they will sort me out. Make me pay,' he replies wearily. 'So, forget about horses that run on time and pubs that open on time. Let's continue with this painting, which is not on time.'

Marilyn once again chided and stared at the leprous wallpaper.

A long few minutes passed.

'Are you married, Lucian?' It was a question she had been bursting to ask but had felt too constrained to do so.

'Yes, yes,' he replied testily. 'Three times so far, so help me.'

'Same here,' says the actress.

'I've got fourteen kids by those women.'

'Wow! Do they come here to the studio? Do you paint them?'

The artist, for once, managed a smile. 'Yes, they do. They have all sat for me when I have needed a model. I paint my assistant now when I need one.'

A few more stained minutes passed. The door ajar allowed a whippet to put its head around the door.

'Oh, you poor dear,' cries the celebrity model.

The dog trots over and licks her toe.

Lucian whacks the weasel with his brush.

'Pluto!'

The dog backs off nervously.

A commotion out on the street is enough to distract the painter.

'Now bloody what?'

A crack on the back window announced a pebble thrown.

'Damn, damn, damn,' he raged like an old master. He stormed to the scene of the intrusion.

Marilyn was already at the front window, only her face visible to those below. She waved to an assembling crowd who were shouting "Marilyn Marlyn".

Lucia opened his window to see a photographer in the garden.

'I want a shot of Marilyn.'

'Fuck off, dwarf.'

The window slammed back down.

He darted back to the other window, opened it, pushing his model to one side.

He roared down at the crowd.

'Go away, go away, you bloody peasants. I am trying to work up here.'

A pitiful plea into the wind. Out of the crowd, making a grand entrance, strode Sir Larry, coat over shoulders, cigarette holder waving majestically.

His audience was silent; he began declaiming.

'Marilyn, Marilyn, once more to the film set, dear Marilyn. You are later than late, my darling. You are keeping the whole production waiting. Your agent and husband are in from the States. Please hurry on down.'

Lucian purple with temper bellowed back.

'Fuck off, you hammy bastard, and take that crew with you. Go on, piss off.'

Back inside, his erstwhile model had quickly dressed, her blue eyes anxious and harassed.

'Oh dear, I'm a social disaster. My analyst cannot cure it. I must go, Lucian. It's been lovely. See you again next week.'

And she was gone. Pluto sniffed after her — he could only blink as his master snapped the big brush in anger. The studio looked so empty, so bare, so grey.

The master sank onto the battered sofa. The master denied — old, cold and browned off.

Pluto came over to lick his hand. He patted the head, raised his own helpless hands and shrugged.

A week later, he sat on the same sofa, a letter in his hand — a rejected suitor, a blown-out lover.
'You get the heave-ho and off you go,' he mutters.
He read the letter to the whippet:

> *'Dear Lucian,*
> *I am sorry, I cannot complete the commission as I have to*
> *return to Hollywood to publicise the picture. I am sure I can sit*
> *for you again next time I'm in England.*
> *Until then, love and kisses,*
> *Marilyn'*

He swore. *'Bollocks. Do I still need a celebrity nude portrait?',* he asked himself.
'Yes, I do.'
For a second, he looked from the letter to the whippet, who looked back without understanding.
'Eureka,' he shouted....
'By jove, I have it. Yes, yes.'
'Kate Moss. Kate Moss.'
'Now there's a real model.'

Tony O'Dwyer
The author, Tony O'Dwyer, wrote this story some years ago.

A Story
By
Maria Irina Popescu

VAMPIRE REVOLUTION

Jon Howard, 29, white, and a Londoner by choice, had been dreaming of vampires for as long as he could remember.

Or, to be more precise, of one vampire in particular.

When néni Sara told stories of cousin Jacques, she never said the word *vampire*, not in English, Hungarian, or French. But Jon understood. Cross-legged on the rug, the heater burning his spine, he listened. He saw an elegant man who bent the world to his will. He no longer heard his parents tear at each other downstairs. When he fell asleep imagining Jacques, Jon didn't wet the bed.

In time, this all fell away. Sara walked into the sun, which turned her into a heap of ash. She had to move into an urn the size of a tissue box. Jon trained as a reporter. He lived, mostly at night. And he forgot.

Until today.

Jon returned to the office after lunch. With the first snowflakes of the season melting on his coat, he spotted a photo on Montgomery's desk. A marble Madonna and child beneath a stone canopy.

Jacques' grin rose in him like steam.

He turned the photo over. *Maria Square, Timişoara, Socialist Republic of Romania.* Jon touched it, leaving a bloody smudge.

A papercut smarted.

The brandy he'd had with lunch ignited inside him. His ungloved fingertips tingled as they thawed.

Paulie's door was shut. Jon didn't knock.

'I can smell you from here,' the editor said without looking up from her papers.

Jon approached anyway. He set the photo in front of Paulie. She pushed it away.

'The American has no connection to this place. I do.'

He leaned across the desk. She glanced at the pale strip of skin that showed where the coat sleeves had ridden up. 'You're still not well.'

He sank his hands into his pockets. The memory of a feeling: a tightrope swaying, his stomach lurching, the darkness below staring back with fiery eyes. The scars on his wrist flickered with pain.

'You can't force me to write reviews forever,' he said.

Paulie sighed. The silver in her cropped curls caught the lamp light. Outside, it was almost evening. Large snowflakes fell quietly.

'Then at least tell me what's happening here.'

The editor took off her glasses and looked at him. Her expression was softer now. 'A Calvinist pastor spoke against Ceaușescu on Canadian radio. Hungarian state media broadcast it. Now he's about to be evicted. His congregation are protesting.'

'It'll blow up. Look what happened in Berlin last month.'

Paulie blinked once. She looked drained. A vein tightened in her neck. Jon's stomach turned. Once he was changed, he'd never feel nausea again.

'What does the American know?' his voice rose. 'You *need* me there. I speak the language. I understand the people.'

The editor scoffed. 'Well, *that's* an overstatement.' Her face hardened. 'It's out of my hands. The visa is in Greg's name. His train's leaving at seven tonight.'

'But Paulie –'

She glared. 'Do you want my advice? Go home and sleep it off. Come back first thing tomorrow and we'll talk about what you can do. From – your – desk.' She punctuated her words with little taps on the desk.

Jon stood there, empty-headed, waiting for a miracle.

Paulie put on her glasses and turned to her papers.

On his way out, Jon made up his mind. If the story belonged to Montgomery, then he'd have to become Montgomery.

At home, Jon kept his coat on. He poured himself another brandy to numb the churning in his stomach. A train rushed by; his shitty windows rattled. He packed a bag. Essentials only: underwear, toiletries. A couple of clean shirts. His dog-eared English-Hungarian pocket dictionary and a new notebook. He slipped a strip of passport photos into his wallet, but left his passport in the drawer.

The 'savings' envelope he kept under the mattress was empty. Hopefully, Paulie had set aside an allowance for the trip.

'Szervusz, néni Sara,' he said out loud as he left the flat. 'I won't be gone long.'

On the mantle, the small urn stayed quiet.

Greg Montgomery looked ridiculous in that trench coat he'd been wearing since September.

Jon walked up the platform, trying to ignore the icy air that clawed through his clothes. It stank of diesel.

'All right?' he said as he stopped by Montgomery's side.

A smile broke on the American's uncomplicated face. 'Jonathan! My man! What are you doing here?' They shook hands.

'Going to visit family. You're off on assignment, I hear.'

Montgomery nodded. 'My first time behind the Iron Curtain. Don't know what to expect. Think it'll be extremely cold?' Still clutching the suitcase handle, the American tightened the belt of his trench coat.

'Absolutely. Beware of vampires, too,' Jon said deadpan.

'Really?' The man's eyes widened.

Jon smiled. 'Say, I don't suppose you fancy a cuppa? I'm awfully early, and it's freezing in here.'

Montgomery hesitated. He checked his wristwatch, checked his train ticket before slipping it back into the trench coat. 'OK,' he said after a whole minute had passed. 'A quick one.'

Some way away from the platform, in the poorly-decorated station café, Jon and Montgomery made small talk. When the American excused himself to use the facilities, Jon waited until he was out of sight, then pinched his colleague's train tickets. In the suitcase, he found maps, an envelope containing mixed currencies (pounds, lizard-hued American dollars, and the local currency, lei), and a folder containing details of a local contact, Szabina Székely.

He wouldn't know what to do with any of this, Jon thought. The American didn't understand. He didn't have Sara to guide him or Jacques.

Jon took it all and left before Montgomery returned.

On the train to Dover, Jon carefully replaced Montgomery's passport photo with his own, slicked his hair back like the man did, and practiced his American accent.

It all felt delicious. Jacques stayed by his side, his playful grin the most pleasant company.

During the ferry crossing, Jon examined Szabina's folder. Her photo showed a mousy girl with a severe fringe and thick glasses. She was Hungarian, like néni Sara, so he looked for his great-aunt's strong nose and prominent cheekbones. He found only a wide, unremarkable face with eyebrows too unruly to be attractive. Such a weakling! A bio described her as a model Communist youth who loved reading, photography, and 'the motherland's exquisite forests.' Jon chuckled.

Over too many drinks in overheated dining cars and uneasy naps in cracked leather seats, Jon fantasised about his impending transcendence into the vampiric realm. He knew he was right this time; he felt it in his gut. If a revolution was indeed coming, he could easily disappear; sooner or later, Paulie would have to stop searching.

As trains crossed the continent, Jacques stayed by his side, reassuring.

Think about it: no more poverty – no more weakness – no more pain.

Néni Sara was there too, in every older woman wrapped in furs, French perfume, and cigarette smoke. Her attention was turned inwards, towards her gilded past, as it had always been.

Not long left to go now.

Bribes seemed less sordid in the woods than in cities, Jon thought as he handed over a neat wad of dollars. The guards (armed, wearing tricolour armbands) didn't even glance at him. They just stamped his passport and waved him through. Jon exhaled a cloud of vapour, thick with relief.

They crossed the border at dusk.

His driver sang along to a muffled cassette of *The Wall*. 'We don't need no e-*du*-ca-*tion*... We don't need no *thought* con-*trol*,' he drummed on the steering wheel, his rebellious smirk reflected in the mirror. Jon smiled. The idea of a song having so much power amused him.

He sang along.

When they reached Timişoara it was darker than he'd expected. Scheduled power outages, the driver said. The Continental was quite empty. A receptionist served him an extravagant dinner: soup, pork, pickles, plum brandy. He ate it all, until his stomach hurt. When the chef appeared to shake his hand, Jon understood they'd mistaken his gratitude for enthusiasm.

Later, in his room, full and drowsy, he stood by the window watching snowflakes settle over the pavement. He felt no connection to this place. The strangeness of it all squeezed at his heart. Was this really where he would die?

No need for melodrama. A new world was right around the corner.

Too early the next morning, the phone rang. 'Miss Székely is here.'

He was half-asleep when he stumbled into the lobby, unshaven and sweating from last night's spirits. The young woman waiting for him wore a sheepskin coat, cropped hair, and huge glasses. She was more expressive than in the photo. An old-fashioned camera hung around her neck. She looked him up and down.

'Has someone been chasing you?' Szabina smirked.

'Only my hopes and dreams,' he said, instantly regretting it.

While he drank a cup of thin-filter coffee, she ate his

breakfast.

'Someone's hungry,' he teased. She ignored him.

They marched in silence through the park, then crossed the river. The sky was lit up by the brightest of suns. A rare treat that Jon will soon miss.

'Where's everyone?' he asked, catching his breath. The freezing air like shards down his airways.

'At work,' Szabina shrugged.

After twenty minutes, they reached Maria Square. Jon recognised the marble mother-and-child statue from the photo.

A small crowd was gathering all around them.

'Do you see that palace?' Szabina said, pointing at the austere corner building past the monument. 'That's the Reformed Church. And up there,' she pointed at an open window on the second floor, 'is where pastor László Tőkés lives. For now.'

'The regime wants him out because he spoke out,' Jon said.

'And because he's Hungarian,' Szabina said.

Jon wondered whether Jacques was ever allergic to churches. 'So it's about religion.'

'No. It's about survival.' She turned to him, squinting in the sun. 'How would you feel if your queen demolished Shakespeare's theatre?' There was provocation in her tone. Jon didn't appreciate it.

'I don't know.'

'You don't have to.' Her voice dropped to a sharp whisper. 'The *Comrade*'s been pouring concrete over our culture for twenty years. Villages flattened, schools closed. People flee. Thousands of Hungarians, Germans, and anyone who can. Whoever's left is barely standing. But this – ' she gestured toward the crowd, 'this means some of us are still awake.'

The protest remained small for most of the day: old men in heavy coats, women with scarves knotted under their chins. Some prayed aloud. Steam rose from their mouths.

'They're Calvinists?' Jon asked.

'Look closer.' Szabina nodded toward the flickering candles, barely visible in the toothy sun. 'Calvinists don't use candles. Those are Orthodox Romanians. They joined too.'

Flames played in tired eyes. It was touching, and ominous, and complicated. Jon wasn't sure of what he felt.

After dark, as soon as work hours ended, more people arrived. Men lit cigarettes instead of candles and spoke in loud voices and spat on the ground.

Szabina told him: 'This happened before. In Cluj, three years ago. Iași, two years ago. Factory employees in cities angry about austerity measures and redundancies. In Brașov ten thousand workers walked out, chanting against the regime. The military got involved, but the penalties weren't too harsh—the state claimed it was an isolated incident. By now, most people know what's going on. They listen to banned radio stations, to Free Europe.'

Jon listened and took notes just to keep his hands from going numb. When she spoke to him, Szabina sounded as matter-of-fact as a dictionary. She had no interest in connecting with him or even speaking to him in her language. She stood very still. Her eyes only came alive when she glanced at the ever-swelling crowd, as she prepared to take a photo.

Take my photo, he wanted to say. It'll be the last one.

She made him feel lonely. He avoided looking at her.

'Why are you so tense? There's no police,' Jon whispered.

She grabbed his arm hard and pulled him back. She glanced over her shoulder. Wrapped in her sheepskin coat, her body stuttered, hypervigilant.

'What's *wrong* with you?' he shouted.

'There *is* police, plenty of them. They're just not in uniform. They're the *Securitate*, the secret police.'

'How do you spell that?'

'Do you think your *Scotland Yard* doesn't?'

Another memory. How long ago was that? Seven, eight years? Jon was at university. Plainclothes officers are stopping and searching young Black men in Brixton for no reason. One stabbed, bleeding. That turned out well.

The noise swelled around them. Instinctively, Jon pulled

Szabina back, but she ignored him again.

'The mayor,' she said, nodding towards the man who had just arrived in front of the crowd. He was flanked by men in long coats.

'No eviction today!' he shouted. 'It's Saturday. Go home!'

'Put it in writing!' someone called back.

The crowd started chanting, 'In writing, in writing! Put it in writing!' Szabina chanted along with them, her camera swaying across her chest.

That's when the pastor appeared at the window. His voice was thin but steady. 'Go home, my friends. Pray for peace.'

No one moved.

Instead, they started chanting, low at first, then rising: '*Libertate! Libertate!*'

Uniformed gendarmes gathered at the edges. Amongst them, Jon could swear he spotted Jacques. He had assumed a disguise to protect his weaker relative – he must've. Now Jon had to find his way across this sea of people to Jacques. He swigged from his hip flask to ignite some courage. Neither Jacques nor the marble Mary blinked.

When the first baton struck, it sounded like nothing. A barely audible dull thud. Then another. Screams followed. Szabina grabbed Jon's arm. 'Move!' she shouted, pulling him away from the eye of the storm.

Someone grabbed a stone and hurled it at an empty-eyed Militia man. As he drove his boots into the first belly he came across, there was pleasure in his grin.

Jon winced, feeling the kick in his own stomach. Yet he freed himself from Szabina's grip and moved forward towards Jacques.

Someone shouted '*Jos Ceaușescu!*' and then they all shouted '*Jos Ceaușescu!*'

'What are you doing?' Szabina shouted in Jon's ear. 'Have you lost your mind?'

He could no longer see the familiar face in the police cordon, but advanced nonetheless against the grain. Szabina squeezed his hand as the crowd jerked them back and forth.

Locked them in her mad embrace.

Up the boulevard, across the river. Drops of icy water lashed Jon's face; landed on Szabina's glasses. 'Water cannons!' the whispers travelled.

Ahead, blood gushed from someone's nose, seeped through another's matted hair. Jon felt his mouth watering.

A piece of metal shaped like a charred angel was carried through the crowd. It, too, longed to transcend its nature.

Rumour spread that crazy men had pried it out of a cannon.

For one singular moment, the crowd retreated like a diseased gum and they watched as three workers, still in their oil-stained overalls, smashed the display window of a shop, grabbed the books on display and tore their pages, and burnt them with matches.

'Not *real* books,' Szabina answered the question in his eyes. 'They're written by *them*,' and Jon understood she meant the two tyrants, the husband and the wife.

'We no longer need them,' she said. 'We're free.'

Then there he was. Jacques. A stone's throw away. In the beautifully stony face, Jon recognised his own forehead, his own temples and brow. It must be him, Jon was certain. He pushed his way closer. 'It's me, cousin,' he shouted. 'It's me. I'm here. I'm ready.'

He was so close that Jon could touch him. But – he stank of exile. His grin was sadistic, not playful. It can't have been him.

A fistful of glass shards forced its way down his mouth and throat. Barbed wire lined his sockets as they tightened and tightened into the squishy globes of his eyes.

Somewhere on a nearby street, a siren blared.

Jon tried to hold his breath, but instead inhaled more broken glass, filling his lungs with it and making it worse. He screwed his eyes shut, and he fell to his knees, right there in the middle of the stream, whimpering.

The pain expanded until it swallowed him and the siren and the crowd whole.

Jacques grabbed Jon by his deflated chest and dragged him through the darkness for a long time, until the white noise in his ears sighed into silence. He had been saved. Jacques poured something thick in Jon's eyes; the pain shrank and began to fall away.

Jon came to the sound of a radio turned low. His skin burned; breathing felt shallow. He was slumped on a stool at a small, oilcloth-covered kitchen table. Was this what *immortality* felt like? A single candle flickering in the darkness, static, and the stink of sulphur?

Two figures moved around him. Both – women? Disappointment felt like a grape drying too quickly into a raisin.

One voice he recognised.

'There you are,' Szabina said brightly.

Jon let out a breath. He hadn't been – he was still human. Trapped with this cold, cold girl. The pungent smell scratched at the back of his throat. He coughed.

'I've already opened the window,' Szabina said. 'Anymore and we'll freeze.'

Blue flames played around all four hob rings.

And he was wrapped in an itchy wool blanket. Beneath it –

'Where are my clothes?' he rasped.

'In the bathtub, soaking,' the second woman said. Her voice was gentle. Jon stared at her long, dark hair, at her unblinking eyes. Hypnotic. Was she a vampire? Had Jacques sent her?

'Why did you charge at that militia man?' Szabina scolded him. 'He tear-gassed you, stupid.'

Jon found nothing to say.

The stranger touched his forehead, then smiled. 'I'm Aurora. Are you warm enough? Here, drink this.'

She handed him a glass. He downed it. Some kind of fruit brandy. She refilled. The liquor spread its fire inside him, loosened the vice around his head.

Outside, fireworks.

'No, not fireworks,' Szabina said. 'Shots. They're firing.'

'Are you sure?' Jon frowned.

'You're staying here tonight,' Aurora told him. She touched his shoulder. 'Perhaps this is the night when hope catches fire. You will tell our story, yes?'

An acidic guilt rose in Jon's throat. How angry must Paulie be by now?

They spent some tense hours huddled in the dark kitchen. They ate cornmeal porridge and cheese, listened to Radio Free Europe describing clashes and incoming tanks. Between bulletins, they played cards.

'You can love your country and still want to be happy,' Aurora said softly, squeezing Szabina's hand, whose expression was more tender than Jon had thought her capable of.

Later, as they slept in the bedroom, he tossed and turned on the sofa. When the busted springs beneath him turned unbearable, he stood up and walked to the window. He stared at the purple sky and down at the city. The roads, the squares, the concrete apartment buildings. Straight down. There, staring back at him, was Jacques, draped in black velvet and brocade.

Jon threw his coat over the pyjamas Szabina had lent him, crammed his feet inside his shoes, and ran down the four flights of stairs. When he made it out, panting and clutching his stomach, Jacques was gone. A single shot tore through the night; a terrible silence bled out of the wound. Jon held his breath.

A second shot. And then a third.

There he was. Across the street. The same playful grin animated his beautifully pale face. Jon followed.

A turn. Shots rang closer.

In the freezing night air, Jon's eyes and heart burned with the excitement of reunion.

Jacques led Jon back to Maria Square, empty except for a plainclothes officer who, under the marble mother's gaze, aimed his pistol at the sky. His clean-shaven cheeks had turned red from the vodka that now sloshed in a thin layer at the bottom of a bottle. Before disappearing, Jacques turned to face Jon. His fiery eyes stared, not unfriendly, while his fingers simulated a gunshot to the head. His mouth formed a playful grin.

Jon understood: if he jumped out of the shadows, he would startle the drunk officer, who'd shoot him before asking questions. This life would end so that a new one would begin. After all this time, Jacques was finally welcoming Jon into his world. One step, and he too could be free.

One step. That was all it took.

But Jon hesitated. He thought of Paulie, of her concern flickering across his scars. He thought of néni Sara, all alone in her tissue-box urn.

'Jon.' A hand touched his shoulder.

He turned. Aurora. Her eyes wet.

'Szabina's gone.'

Jon didn't understand.

'Her camera's missing. I thought she'd come back here.'

He looked out onto the square. Jacques was gone. The drunk militia man was kneeling in front of Mary, clutching the pistol as his hands joined in prayer.

'There's no one here,' Jon whispered. 'No one except – him.'

Aurora squeezed his arm. 'Help me find her, please.'

He took one step, then stopped. The sound of Aurora's breath in his ear made him feel more real than he'd ever felt.

Jon Howard had been dreaming of vampires for as long as he could remember. And he still was. He knew that Jacques was out there, haunting the night. But so was Szabina. So were they. And so was freedom.

Maria Irina Popescu

THREE SHORT STORIES, TWO FLASH-FICTIONS AND ONE POEM
By
Rosemary Watson

LIGHTENING

A Story For Children

'Come along,' Mum said.

Dawn's broken alarm went off, and soon the chorus of a busy day ahead began, which heralded the take-off time for my little darlings.

'But Mum,' said the male child of the family, 'I'm really afraid to fly.'

'This is your time, your destiny,' said Dad as the family left the comfort of their cosy home and set out in good time for the impending take-off. 'This is only a domestic flight, very short, to prepare you for the long journey you will soon take to warmer climes and meet up with family and old friends.'

The journey to the take-off point was within walking distance of their home, but it was slow and tiring. However, the family made good time, especially after passing family, friends and neighbours who offered their good wishes and greetings for the day's adventure.

Arriving in good time for the flight and as the family stood patiently waiting in line for their call to be airbourne, they heard the usual, 'I'm thirsty, I'm hungry' chatter of the little ones. The wise parents knew the score and kept their resolve, having experienced the same fears not long ago.

Just as the family prepared for take-off, a burst of thunder clapped loudly in the air, and from their high vantage point of the tower, they all automatically looked up as the storm broke with the dawn.

'Oh no!' said the parents, whispering to each other.

They put on a brave face to the little ones; they fondly reassured them that it was nothing to be afraid of.

The rain fell, but they were under the safe cover of the departure point, so they calmly commenced the procedure they had practised many times before today.

By the time the flight was taking off, the little ones saw the wings go up and at last began to relax and enjoy the experience.

The thunder raged, and the storm was fierce, away from the safety of the departure point.

With a radiance illuminating the sky, a flash of such incandescence discharged its power, lighting up the sky with luminosity that startled the airborne family.

'Target the light in the sky,' said the leader of The Attack as he flashed his weapons of mass destruction at the oncoming brightness. A strong partisan near the front of the line of fire could see the peering small faces frightened at their "in-flight". Being of a rather more empathic nature than the leader of the pack, held back from the "unquestioning orders" from the Mighty One and directed the energy of the "pack" to the left of the light.

The leader relayed "next target" to his crew as they crawled across to an unsuspecting break in the clouds where the sun was trying to break free.

'What's that in the sky?' said the little male child to his father, now ecstatically airborne.

'Nearly there,' said Dad, 'End of the rainbow where the sun is.'

As the family landed and the little ones shook their feathers, feeling brave but exhausted, the partisan member of the attack smiled and cackled with pleasure. His rebellious nature felt satisfaction as the family he had saved was enveloped in safe wings wrapped around each other.

The End

Rosemary Watson

GRIEF

Never Take Things For Granted

This unconventional poem structure expresses feelings after watching I Swear, a film that follows a character with Tourette's Syndrome:

Apart from two people at the back of the cinema, I watched the film alone near the front.

I swear, the effect was physical with my vision blurred as tears spilt and my stomach contracted, as if a punch had hit me. My memory drifted back fifty years, to a time when the smell of fear was just as fierce then as now, but the ignorance evoked the same sense of love and protection I felt in this world.

The protagonist was replaced by an image I could draw upon as if it were yesterday, timeless. The ending of *I Swear* was more positive than the gut-wrenching ending of my own reality. Yet, strangely, the ending brought tears and relief, as grief was once more returned to its quiet resting place within my own heart and mind.

The End

Rosemary Watson

RICHARD III

"Freytag's Pyramid" is a storytelling framework that breaks a narrative into five staged: exposition, rising action, climax, falling action, and resolution. "Richard III" uses this framework and is based on a fairy tale in the style of Hansel and Gretel. The flash fiction story uses a bio-fiction structure, merging fact with fiction. The narrator is the voice of King Richard III at The Holy Cross Priory, New Walk, Leicester:

I have been buried for centuries, awaiting the discovery of my broken bones in this place of battle, Leicester, the heart of England.

A Roman Catholic requiem mass for me with these chosen people who have kept the faith —how beautiful are the hymns and the colourful manner of their dress. This is progress, and now I can, at last, be laid to rest in peace.

I was wrongly accused of treachery by my nephews, and as a result, they ordered that I be murdered. I was made to fight for my life by being cast adrift by my own family and found safety and solace away from the shores of England.

This is not a fairy story. This is not Cinderella. More like Hansel and Gretel, and here at my very own funeral, I can lay the records straight.

The End

Rosemary Watson

MAGICAL REALM

A Lady having her nails painted looks down at her hands, tipped in tar.

Maria was enticed into the tent at the Festival where the aromatic smells escaped from the flap.

Today it's feet or hands massaged, then nail polish applied for only £10, as written on the poster in purples, violets, indigo and lilac.

'See you in 20 minutes,' called Maria to her fellow festival-goers.

The smells of burning incense and the low, comfortable seating, coupled with the gentle voice of the veiled therapist, soon had Maria slipping into a trance-like dream.

'Is this the colour you have chosen?' was a distant voice, as she felt herself in a whirlpool like a rollercoaster at the funfair.

Landing in a pool of soft sticky substance made Maria try to bring her mind into this different environment and not panic. Her beautiful purple-painted nails were now coated in a sticky, tar-like substance.

Crawling along slowly, a glimpse of a light appeared, from what could be some tunnel.

As the light became brighter, a whoosh of air hit her face, and she emerged from the tunnel to a seaside. This is surreal as the Festival is nowhere near the sea! Panicking, she tried to imagine her friends trying to find her.

'Wait, there are people on the sand with banners. I will try to reach them for help and to escape from this madness.'

NO OIL HERE came into her focus as she crawled towards the banner carriers.

A ship in the distance completed the picture on the beach, but a ship nearer to "The People" made Maria call out in horror and disbelief.

Goul-like creatures covered in the same sticky tar as she was marched along the beach, holding their banners up high.

The strength that came from getting back to the cave and the tunnel was surreal. Then, as she saw the end of the whirlpool disappearing into the sandy, tar-like substance, she crawled back into the water and swam up the fast-flowing rapids.

Emerging from the tent, she heard the therapist call her name as her friends waited.

Ashen-faced, she headed home with her friends, and that evening she joined Action to Stop Oil on social media.

Looking down at her manicure and nail gel, there were only short nails coloured in an oily blue.

The End

Rosemary Watson

WITCHES

This story considers how mythology influences characterisation. It continues from a visual prompt during a creative writing class – a Witch with a boy and a girl leaving her cottage, clutching a piece of bread. The influences are Video of Witches (2015), Film (2023), and The Little Mermaid from the perspective of an outsider about a character:

Melanie had felt like a foreigner—an outsider—for most of her life. As she was given the keys to her lovely, brand-new home, a new feeling of belonging brought her joy and a spring in her step. Being the first to take up residence, she busied herself with new curtains and making the house into a home where she could relax and enjoy her family and friends.

As Melanie's first neighbour moved in, she made an effort to make him welcome, knowing how it felt to move to a new country —or, indeed, to a new part of the country. The man reminded her of pictures she had seen of what the devil looks like. Short, stocky build, didn't smile, and the big bulbous nose completed the picture. Offering a friendly greeting and asking if there was anything she could help with was not met with a smile, but she put that down to him just finding his feet and adjusting to his new abode.

Apart from grumbling about the dividing fencing and getting his dog out for a walk, nothing foretold the evil that would explode when the neighbour moved into the third house.

Having grown up with tales of witches and fairies, as well as religious stories, an angel came in many guises just when you needed them, especially your Guardian Angel and all were called upon when the Witch arrived in need of a coven.

Full of boasting, strife, jealousy, violence, and madness, the new neighbour appeared, making her ugly persona on the newly laid drives and lawn. Melanie could only look out her window and think about Macbeth's witches, and yes, she had a cat. "How can I get around this?"

The design of the homes was that she would need to pass The Witch on her way in and out on foot and by car. Best to try to be welcoming and friendly!

A cackle was her response, and so she decided to ignore The Witch and enjoy her new surroundings.

After several attempts, the Devil himself managed to get an opening to go inside the Witch's house, and this is where they plotted and schemed to complete their takeover.

Visitors, family, and good-meaning friends could not prevent the war they waged against their supposed enemy! Dirty, ugly, disease-ridden, lying and contemptuous evil was their craft.

Battle lines were drawn as they opened their box of madness, gossip, hatred and dirty evil in the new neighbourhood.

A box of bravery was smashed open as every scrap of patience and tenacity was used to fight the foes. As their very convincing behaviours were finally laid bare, the white witch deprived them, very slowly, of their behaviours.

When a stooped figure emerged from the house, clutching bread in his hand, Melanie was reminded of the picture of the witch from her childhood. She searched for her old school books, and there it was in a box that had been unopened until she came across it when packing to move home.

The End

Rosemary Watson

ABSTRACT ART

The remit of this writing piece involved a film called The Witches and a film about an underwater witch in The Little Mermaid. This piece includes something the writer had been dreaming about, offering another perspective on the earlier 'Witches' story: This story of the witches was written into a fable involving devils and white and black witches, leaving the writer, Caroline, with a dream of being surrounded by them and of a rescue!

The dreams faded as the next week she had to wander down an art gallery and choose an abstract painting that appealed to her. There he was, the man in her dreams?

The abstract setting made the figure indistinguishable at first, but then the blue background, denoting calmness and responsibility, coupled with a red, passionate torso, splashes of yellow, red, and green, offering a new beginning of vitality and abundance, drew the writer to this painting.

The male figure was sitting astride a rock, maybe?

As Caroline looked again, that evening, at the picture on her phone, she put the photo alongside the poster of The Little Mermaid, and there was Javier Bardem, as King Neptune, astride a rock. He had to let his daughter go to her true love on land after defeating the evil sorceress under the sea.

Caroline had been in awe of Javier for over twenty years and had watched all his films; yes, he was her Hero.

The dreams that weekend were of all types of horror, with Javier coming to the rescue.

Selecting the story of the Witches and then the Rescuer for her chosen pieces to present made Caroline dream of happier times in the past and maybe in the future?....

The End

Rosemary Watson

A DARK COMEDY SERIES OVERVIEW AND EPISODE
By
Emma Astra

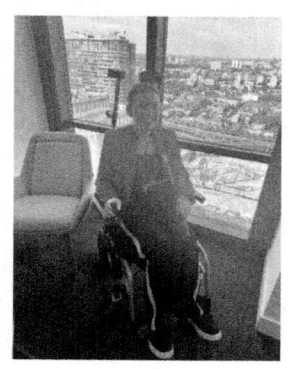

TALES FROM THE HOSPITAL WARD SERIES OVERVIEW

What My Submission to the Book Includes
My contribution to *Pen Pal Tales Book Two – Winter Edition* brings together two connected pieces that blend fiction, research, and reflection:

1. **This Series Overview & Episode Guide** — introducing *Tales from the Hospital Ward,* its origins, characters, and themes, with links for further reading. For example, discussion and links are provided for you to read free Episodes 1-3, a Reflective Essay, a Research/newspaper-style article about hospital stays for people with inflammatory bowel disease, and a presentation article that includes a video and a behind-the-scenes process that links the project together.

2. **A Special Christmas & New Year Fiction** — Two linked short stories ("Crackers and Transparent Gravy" and "Buzzers and Fireworks") continue the *Tales from the Hospital Ward* (Episode 4) series in festive chaos, especially produced for this anthology and relevant to the book's "winter" theme.
   These pieces show how creative writing, lived experience, and investigative storytelling can coexist; using humour, honesty, and data to bridge fiction and real life.

Series Overview & Episode Guide
Introduction
Tales from the Hospital Ward is a **fictional** series based on my experiences as a patient on a gastroenterology ward in Leicester. The ward specialises in digestive diseases, particularly Inflammatory Bowel Disease.
   The stories draw on real life but anonymise every name and scene for the sake of safeguarding and confidentiality. The writing

looks back to 2020 for Episodes 1 to 3—the height of the pandemic —when chronic-illness care was sidelined and every corridor felt suspended in time. I wasn't admitted for COVID, but for ulcerative colitis-related disease, which is similar to Crohn's. Yet the atmosphere of exhaustion, improvisation, and humour that carried the NHS through that year became my setting. I wanted to capture compassion and absurdity side by side and write it with the audience in mind, being an avid TV watcher myself.

How It Began

The series began during my practice-based PhD, *The Diary of a Disabled PhD Student: Sharing Lived Experience of Chronic Illness and Disability Using Digital Media and Journalism.* (https://doi.org/10.25392/leicester.data.28730849).

My research explored whether fiction could sometimes tell the truth more safely than autobiography — revealing experience without re-traumatising those who lived it. This insight became the ethical backbone of the whole series — each episode tells the truth safely, without exposing real identities. Writing became both therapy and inquiry, transforming pain into a creative method.

Process and Development

Because of dyslexia, dyspraxia, and fluctuating health, I drafted by voice-to-text and edited manually. I wrote episodes 1-3 during 2023-2024, approximately two years into my PhD and three years after the events in those episodes. I circulated it to friends in my creative writing class, who encouraged me to continue developing the series. This accessibility-first process reflects Pen Pals Publishing's ethos of inclusive creative practice.

The first three episodes were published on online writing platforms *Substack* and *Medium* as "living drafts," open for readers to follow the process and the story.
Each republication traced my own recovery — creative, physical, and social.

When I later co-founded Pen Pals Publishing with other

Leicester writers from the same class, the series became an example of how creative writing and lived-experience research can be combined to create accessible, socially relevant storytelling. Encouraged by classmates who became co-founders of Pen Pals, I returned to the series for our second anthology, adding a brand-new Christmas & New Year Special.

From Pandemic to Aftermath

The new festive double episode advances the timeline.

Whereas the early stories captured the first lockdown's fear and stillness, these new ones show what lingers: staff burnout, shifting priorities, small absurdities that become the new normal. COVID is no longer named, but its fingerprints are everywhere — in shortages, paperwork, and the fragile humour people use to cope. An era which continues and is now called 'Post-COVID'.

The Setting

The ward is fictional but rooted in Leicester Royal Infirmary's gastroenterology ("gastro") hospital wards in the United Kingdom. For the publication, the ward is renamed Leicester High Hospital. "Ward 101" stands for countless NHS bays: fluorescent lights, meal trolleys, and curtains that never quite close. Leicester is the series' heartbeat — diverse, working-class, and unpretentious.

Following the influence of late Leicester author Sue Townsend's writing, I aim to use local humour and everyday speech to make social commentary feel human. Place becomes a character: a city that refuses pity, finding laughter in bureaucracy.

Episode Guide
Episode 1 — Watchful Eye

Introduces the narrator and the ward during early 2020: observation, fear, and the uneasy silence of isolation.

Original Version (20.12.2023):
https://disabledphdstudent.substack.com/p/tales-from-the-hospital-ward-part?
utm_source=substack&utm_campaign=post_embed&utm_medi
um=web

Republished Version 2 (1.10.2025):
https://medium.com/creative-writing-hub/tales-from-the-hospital-ward-b0df1435acc3

Episode 2 — Morphine, Bottles, and the Red Buzzer
Humour and frustration collide in a sleepless night of alarms, painkillers, and compassion under pressure.
Original Version (18.2.2024):
https://disabledphdstudent.substack.com/p/tales-from-the-hospital-ward-episode?
utm_source=substack&utm_campaign=post_embed&utm_medi
um=web
Republished Version 2 (1.10.2025):
https://medium.com/creative-writing-hub/tales-from-the-hospital-ward-33f1588d155a

Episode 3 — Monday 9 pm (BBC 1)
A meta-episode imagining the ward as a primetime drama, exposing how patients perform resilience while hiding fear.
Original Version (23.3.2024):
https://disabledphdstudent.substack.com/p/tales-from-the-hospital-ward?
utm_source=substack&utm_campaign=post_embed&utm_medi
um=web
Republished Version 2 (1.10.2025):
https://medium.com/creative-writing-hub/tales-from-the-hospital-ward-2cc46b95eddf

Festive Double Episode — Christmas & New Year Special (2025)
The following two stories form the festive double episode written especially for this Winter Edition of *Pen Pal Tales* (*Crackers and Transparent Gravy* and *Buzzers and Fireworks*). You don't have to read the previous episodes for the ones in this book to make sense. Each episode can be read as a stand-alone piece, just like watching an episode of *Casualty*, but set on a gastroenterology ward rather than in A&E, offering a different and patient-led perspective.
The pandemic backdrop fades; routine chaos replaces crisis and

a more "Post-Covid" era. Plastic-wrapped "crackers," collapsing bedpans, a clock date that never tells the right day.

Through humour and heartbreak, the stories reveal how the extraordinary becomes ordinary.
Online Version (8.10.2025):
https://medium.com/creative-writing-hub/tales-from-the-hospital-ward-christmas-new-year-special-17d1e9872ca7

Character Overview
Main Series Characters (Episodes 1–3)
(Set during the 2020 pandemic period)

The Narrator (Patient) — Observer and anchor; wry, empathetic, documenting the thin line between care and chaos — yet fully aware of her own flaws, ironies, and contradictions, like most humans trying to make sense of themselves and others. The reader never gets to hear their name.

Chelsea (Patient) — Loud, restless, unpredictable. Orders a taxi to Morrisons, meets her drug dealer outside, and smuggles takeaways back in. A mixture of comic energy and underlying pain.

Jade (Patient) — Keeps vodka bottles hidden in her bedside bag. Her humour and rebellion mask fear and loneliness; her clinking bottles echo through every episode.

Edna (Patient) — Initially misdiagnosed with dementia instead of a water infection until Health Care Assistant (HCA) Sarah intervenes. Later suffers burns from an ileostomy-bag leak — a haunting image of neglect and systemic failure.

Sarah (HCA) — Compassionate and alert; spots Edna's real diagnosis and saves her from a care-home mistake. Represents the practical intelligence and empathy of Health Care Assistants, who are unqualified nurses who assist them with their duties.

Dr Smith (Consultant) — Authoritative and distant; signs Chelsea's discharge after her Morrisons escapade. Embodies clinical detachment and the overstretched, risk-averse system.

Nurse Vicky (Staff Nurse) — Sarcastic, disengaged, forever dreaming of her next all-inclusive holiday. Symbol of fatigue turned cynicism.

Housekeeper (Staff) — Unnamed yet vital; pushes the meal trolley, dispenses gossip, and keeps morale afloat in the background.

Festive Special Characters (Christmas & New Year Episode for this anthology)
(Set later, in the post-pandemic aftermath)

The Narrator (Patient) — Returns older and more reflective, still blending humour with empathy as chaos unfolds around her, but as always with flaws.

Zoe (HCA) — Hard-working and moral heart of the ward; shoulders everyone else's load while still finding grace and gallows humour in chaos.

Maz (Senior Nurse) — Obsessed with breaks and forms; her detachment mirrors burnout and bureaucratic survival mode.

Jane (Nurse) — Loud, cynical, and prejudiced. Her hypocrisy about "no abuse" policies exposes institutional cruelty and everyday racism.

Stella (Nurse) — A gentle Filipino nurse who endures Jane's bullying with quiet dignity — the embodiment of compassion and professionalism.

Gertrude (Patient) — Elderly, deaf, and endearing. Her misheard remarks bring humour and heartbreak; her death on Boxing Day marks a turning point.

June (Patient) — Replaces Gertrude; sharp, outspoken, and lucid yet labelled "abusive" for challenging staff. Died of sepsis after being mis-categorised as a dementia case.

Chelsea (Patient) — Reappears briefly, unchanged — all bravado and brittle defiance.

Jade (Patient) — Still the "party patient," her clinking bottles provide the soundtrack of coping.

Dave (Maintenance Worker) — The comic "clock fixer" who never fixes the clock; emblem of NHS bureaucratic absurdity.

Together, across all four episodes, the cast forms a rotating ecosystem of patients seeking dignity and staff juggling humanity with hierarchy — a community stitched together by pain, humour, and survival instinct. The high number of characters shows the hustle and bustle of real hospital life and the number of people — staff and patients —who experience it daily.

Themes and Tone
Humour as Coping – Black comedy mirrors real ward life.
Empathy & Isolation – Friendships form in fluorescent light.
Systemic Critique – Paperwork meets pain; hierarchy meets humanity.
Representation & Accessibility – Written through a disabled/ chronic illness lens, using plain language for inclusivity.
Leicester Identity – Local wit and working-class realism.
Evolving Time Frame – From pandemic crisis to post-pandemic survival.

Extending the Series — From Fiction to Fact
After completing the festive special, I wrote a companion newspaper-style research article titled "IBD Is Not Just IBS." It uses Freedom of Information data and existing public information to examine hospital food, ward design, and the cost of long IBD stays — the real-world issues behind the fiction. Such examples show how creative writing and journalism can collaborate: one sparks empathy; the other argues for change.

I then created a presentation article that acted as an anchor piece to the series. It included a video and slides, bringing the project together with a behind-the-scenes insight and a full guide with links to each component of the series. The result bridges imagination and evidence, proving that research can live through narrative.

Newspaper /Research article online link (15.10.2025):
https://medium.com/@emmaastra/ibd-is-not-just-ibs-bf93b7a1d32b

Reflective essay online link (8.10.2025):
https://medium.com/creative-writing-hub/tales-from-the-

hospital-ward-a-reflective-essay-cc2e6868d8cf

Presentation article (including slides and video) link bridging the project together (20.10.2025):
https://open.substack.com/pub/emmaastra/p/tales-from-the-hospital-ward?
r=3zdnub&utm_campaign=post&utm_medium=web&showWelc
omeOnShare=false

Looking Ahead — Reflections and Creative Method
After finishing the hospital series, and beginning the **Reflective Essay** and the **presentation** article, I explored the process, inspiration, and *friendship as a method* — how *Pen Pals Publishing* turned shared learning into published work.

I've realised that the best of my writing comes when I lose all inhibition — not through recklessness but honesty. Encouragement from such good friends who formed Pen Pals has, in turn, encouraged me to pursue the series and other creative pieces. In contrast, before, I would lose interest due to apathy within the academic community.

Some writers say to edit ruthlessly; others say to separate the writer from the editor entirely. I've found that for me, writing and editing are the same thing — a kind of dance between clarity and chaos. For example, it's like being that 30-year-old version of yourself in a nightclub, snogging a random guy. The next day, you might regret it, give yourself the ick, or squirm — and sometimes you might be lucky to feel satisfaction. Either way, those moments become stories — for your future self and for others. That's how I approach writing and publishing now: uninhibited, real, slightly messy, but honest enough to mean something. You can always edit at any point down the line. The story stays pure. I discuss these perspectives more in my biography and in the "What Winter Means to Me" section at the end of the book.

Purpose and Impact
My goal is simple: to show that storytelling can now be part of research and reform. Creative writing can also be part of a positive

revolution. In recent years, there has been a surge of books and essays by medical professionals sharing what life in medical settings is like — and while those voices are important, they often tell only half the story.

My take comes from the **patient's perspective** — from the other side of the curtain, the wheelchair, and the iPhone. By centring on the patient's perspective, it complements the professional accounts often seen in medical memoirs.

Tales from the Hospital Ward turns lived experience into narrative evidence—a creative way to understand care, inequality, and resilience. By merging fiction, journalism, and community publishing, I hope to make space for voices in public conversations about health—not as statistics but as storytellers.

Access and Further Reading
If you are reading the eBook version, all pieces discussed in this summary that contribute to *The Tales of the Hospital Ward* series project can be read for free via the links provided. If you're holding the **paperback**, visit:

www.linktr.ee/emmaastra

There you will find all *Tales from the Hospital Ward* episodes, The Reflective Essay, Newspaper/research article, and the presentation link—all free to read.

Closing Note
Whether fiction or fact, all these pieces come from the same ward, the same woman, and the same wish — to make readers feel less alone in the chaos. They aim to raise awareness of the debilitating nature of Inflammatory Bowel Disease and to provoke real, positive change for all involved, including medical professionals, patients, and their families. Because sometimes humour is the only painkiller left — and writing is how we share the dose. A special Xmas and New Year *Tales from the Hospital Ward* is as follows.

Emma Astra

TALES FROM THE
HOSPITAL WARD
Christmas & New Year Special

Series Note

Tales from the Hospital Ward is a **fictional** series based on the author's lived experiences as a patient on a gastroenterology ward in a large UK hospital.

All characters and events are fictionalised for the sake of safeguarding and confidentiality. The following continues the series in the post-pandemic period, capturing the strange calm and chaos of a hospital Christmas. Character and synopsis details are on the previous pages.

Christmas Day on Ward 101 — "Crackers and Transparent Gravy"

(Episode 4, Part 1 of 2)

If you've followed the series, you'll know there are four of us in this bay, with four bays and four side rooms across the ward. The nurses' desk is now as far away from the patients as the eye can see — down a long, million-pound "mobile unit," marketed as innovative and patient-led. Few patients ever make it to the end of that corridor, even with nurses leading the way.

'Do you get triple time on your contract?' Maz asks Zoe in our bay while tapping into her iPad.

'Nah, because we're permanent staff, we don't get all those perks like you lot. You're so lucky,' Zoe replies, turning the sheets.

Maz looks up from her screen. 'All right, Gertrude, I'm going on my break now. Zoe and Shivani are covering your bay for the rest of their shift while I do paperwork.'

'What, love?' Gertrude adjusts her hearing aid. A piercing screech fills the air.

'Bloody hell, what's that noise?' Chelsea screeches back. We all know exactly what it is, but we're signalling to the staff to help Gertrude sort out her hearing aid.

Maz shuffles out as though she never heard a thing.

The bay lights are on full beam; Zoe's Clarks-style shoes squeak on the floor tiles as she turns to the next bed.

Rustle, rustle, from Chelsea's bed area, with her hair in a messy bun, I think they call it these days. Her hair is certainly wild and messy, like her life. Chelsea is frantically rummaging through all her bed space and looks up whilst her hair rocks on the top of her head.

'Where's my phone?' Chelsea looked pissed off, like her life had ended — until she found her phone again, and life was restored.

'Right, I'm going outside for a fag. You coming, Jade?' Chelsea announces, as if we all care deeply.

Gertrude begins her life story for the next hour while Zoe makes all the beds, cleans up Jade's mess from her booze episode, directs the housekeeper, and dishes out everyone's dinners. Shivani is nowhere to be seen, so Zoe works straight through her break.

I repeat for the fourth time that I'm in pain and haven't had any meds. Poor Zoe repeats that she's waiting for Maz, the only one allowed to administer them.

Chelsea and Jade breeze back about five hours later — just as Maz reappears. I'm not sure where the weed smell is coming from.

An hour later, Chelsea announces she's picking up her Deliveroo outside. I guess that answers the question. I heard that cannabis makes people hungry.

'I'm starving, going on my dinner break,' Maz announces.

The look Zoe gives says exactly what I'm thinking: *You just went on your break. And I am now questioning if the weed smell was from Chelsea after all.*

While Maz enjoys what must be her fifth "dinner break," Zoe lets rip.

'We're permanent, yet do all the work, and get paid less for it!'

'WHEN IS BEDTIME?' Gertrude bellows, mishearing the mood.

Zoe dishes out dinner: rubber chicken and mashed-up vegetables.

'Oh, we don't normally have yorkshire puddings with roasts. I ordered fish pie,' groans Jade from her pillow, after downing her second vodka bottle in the bathroom. *Chime, chime, chime* go her bottles behind the thin blue curtain, translucent as the gravy.

We all look confused because every tray has the same thing, each topped with one of those plastic "Ritz-style" lids — or is it the Blitz I'm thinking of? Underneath sit the usual festive extras: a plastic pack with three cream crackers and a triangle of sweaty cheese.

I'm also supposed to be on a low-residue, liquid-only diet, so I've no idea how I ended up with sticky toffee pudding and custard.

'It's Christmas Day!' shouts a random staff member we've never seen.

'It says December twentieth on the clock,' Zoe replies, like butter wouldn't melt.

'It's wrong. Has been for a year. No one's fixed it. It *is* the 25th,' Jade slurs.

'That's why I'm here,' says a man appearing through the bay doors with a screwdriver and drill — but no battery.

'Bloody hell, we do get triple time then,' Zoe mutters; I've never heard her swear before.

All I could think was, *Who wraps three crackers in plastic?* It's not *quite the Christmas "cracker" we expected.*

We learn that the man fixing (or trying to fix) the clock's date is Dave. He spends half an hour telling us about his wife's Christmas dinner and how he's timed his shift perfectly to avoid washing up. When he leaves, the clock still shows 20th December.

As Dave leaves, his timesheet falls out of his pocket: "10 am– 6 pm fixing clock to ensure patient safety and wellbeing." *That's interesting, I thought. He had only been here two hours,* but I said nothing.

So the four of us lay sweating on polyester sheets and equally sweaty plasticky mattresses — Jade's stained, Chelsea's covered in takeaway, Gertrude's with squealing hearing aids, and me complaining about pain. Zoe holds the place together while Maz does paperwork somewhere well away from any patient. Shivani's "on duty" from home, and Christmas spirit tastes of cardboard, Yorkies, watery gravy, and plastic-wrapped cheese and crackers.

The ward's fluorescent lights seem even brighter the darker it gets outside, and begin to hum like a choir. Christmas Day survived.

End of Christmas Day Episode.

New Year's Eve on the Gastro Ward — "Buzzers and Fireworks"
(Episode 4, Part 2 of 2)

A week later, the decorations are drooping. The air smells of sh*t and apathy rather than disinfectant and half-deflated hope.

'Where's the deaf lady gone?'

Oh God — it's that loud-mouth nurse, Jane.

'She died on Boxing Day,' Zoe calls through the bay doors.

'Hello, June! I thought you were Gertrude then — that'll never do, will it?' Jane laughs, seeing to June, who's taken Gertrude's old bed.

'What's that, love?' June says like she's just come out of a hair salon, with short dyed brown hair that's been in rollers all night, giving tight fixed curls, like she just stepped out of a Marilyn Monroe film set.

'YOU'RE STILL AS DEAF AS GERTRUDE THOUGH, AREN'T YOU, JUNE?' Jane booms.

'I'm not deaf! I'm in for my guts,' June says matter-of-factly.

'Yes, your Crohn's,' Jane replies, while June shakes her head.

I'm thinking June hasn't even got the same hairstyle as Gertrude, who was grey.

Zoe brings paper bedpans — made of paper these days, supposedly more hygienic and quicker for staff — which can be binned, rather than the old-fashioned sterilising.

'It's all hands on deck today. The housekeeping team's at a New Year's party, so we're doing everything.'

Maz appears. 'This isn't fair. Expecting us to do the donkey work.'

'I know. They told me I'd be "Band Seven" by now,' Jane adds.

'Haven't you been here decades?' Maz looks around enough to say she doesn't want to be there.

'Yeah, but I was an HCA for years before they trained me. I'm worse off tax-wise now. Should've stayed an HCA — just not worth it.'

While Jane looks away, June soaks the sheets. The paper bedpan goes all mushy, like papier-mâché, which doesn't set.

'Oh, look at that, June — you've got wee everywhere!'

'Well, you shouldn't have looked away, nurse.'

I like June having the guts to say that. She's got guts — physically and literally.

'Now we do not tolerate abuse, June,' Jane snaps, scribbling on her iPad.

'I'm not abusing you! How the heck did you become a nurse? Back when I trained to be a nurse, we had bedside manner.'

'I doubt you were a nurse, June.' Jane looks at others, sniggering, wanting others to join in.

I think *you're right, June*, but again, I say nothing. Maybe I am too ill. Or too scared.

Jane looks towards Zoe again.

'Zoe, check if June has dementia on record — I can't find it.'

'No, nothing like that,' Zoe replies.

'Get the psych team. We can't stand for this nonsense. Staff shouldn't come to work to be abused. Alfred in Bay One bit me earlier!' Jane bellows with her usual abruptness, whilst getting someone else to clean June's wee.

'Alf's got dementia, Jane. Psych team aren't back till January third.'

'Dementia or no Dementia. Its no excuse! We should not be abused!'

Jane's shouting wakes Chelsea.

'Crikey. I recognise that messy bun anywhere. It's you again! Been here five times this year?' Jane says, looking towards Chelsea.

'Not seen you since I've been here this time, though,' Chelsea replies, like they're old mates.

'Been on a Caribbean cruise — all-inclusive. Didn't want to come back to work!' Jane grins whilst carrying on talking, quite a difficult thing to master, I'm thinking,

'So, you still on the wacky-baccy, Chelsea?'

I can't believe Jane asked that.

Chelsea flusters; Jade starts her own "party", bottles clunking behind the curtain.

'Supposed to be good for medical purposes, apparently,' Zoe adds to make Chelsea feel less embarrassed. But most likely covering Jane's backside in case of complaints.

Later, Chelsea puts on lipstick. 'Right, it's party day! I'm off to Morrisons', as she puts her lippy back in her glittery bag.

'Not the corner shop?' Jade asks.

'Nah, booze is cheaper at Morrisons.' Red lippy and phone secured in her bag. Quicker than you could say 'Booze to a shop', Jade gathers her stuff.

'Yeah, all right, I'll come.'

Off they go in an Uber to Morrisons for midnight supplies, still in their pyjamas.

Eight o'clock. The buzzer sounds.

'Filipino, turn that racket off,' Jane orders the new nurse.

'I don't know where the switch is,' Stella replies.

'How long have you been here?' Jane sniggers; staff laugh; patients too. Maybe because Jade and Chelsea are now well drunk.

Stella rushes around like an ant — the kindest nurse here.

'She's bloody useless, that one,' Jane says in front of

everyone.

'Hang on,' June cuts in, 'I thought abuse wasn't allowed... or racism.'

'Now, June, the psych team is coming soon. We don't want your nonsense. Racism is a serious allegation — I'll call the police if you're not careful.'

June's glare says everything.

'We've all done diversity training and signed the equality charter,' Zoe adds, loyal to nurse Jane.

When the clocks strike twelve, most staff have gone. Chelsea and Jade are outside smoking, and meeting Chelsea's drug dealer come-on-off boyfriend. Just me and June remain in the bay.

June turns her head on the pillow.

'She's only jealous of Stella, you know.'

'What?' I ask, wanting to return to my Eastenders New Year's Eve special on my iPad, but too polite to say that.

'Jane. She's jealous. Jane's a bitch. Met plenty of her type in my life.'

The next day, June is transferred to the dementia ward — though she's the sanest person I've met. She dies soon after of sepsis because the staff there never realised she had Crohn's, despite her telling them twenty times and her family writing it down.

End of New Year's Episode.

Epilogue — Ward 101, January 1st
As I am lying here, looking out of the window. Well, not exactly looking out, because the windows need a good wash. But anyway, glaring out towards the packed, overpriced car park, where the frost still lingers, and that's also showing behind the windows, with a queue of ambulances waiting to get into the A&E department opposite Ward 101.

Leftover cardboard Yorkies and plastic crackers litter the floor, along with sh*t around the toilet — because, as the cleaner tells us, they've been told they can't clean bodily fluids for "health and safety reasons." Whether it gets cleaned up depends on the nurse assigned to your bay, which means maybe we will be waiting until next year.

My New Year's Resolution is to campaign to ensure the NHS continues during my lifetime — but, on the other hand, to never come back here, because I fear my life would be in danger.

Series Links & Further Reading
More *Tales from the Hospital Ward* episodes can be found on Medium and Substack:
https://www.linktr.ee/emmaastra

Emma Astra

ABOUT THE AUTHORS

Picture of the co-founders and contributors of Pen Pal Tales and Publishing.

Anne Connue

I was born and raised in Leicester but moved away to be a teacher. However, I've never lost touch with Leicester as my family live here. My mum was a Leicester lady, with family from Leicestershire and Rutland. My dad's family were from Kent, Sussex, Cardiff, and the West Midlands, but he himself was born and raised in India.

All this gives me plenty of Family History to use in my stories. I also enjoy general history, classical music (both listening to and singing it), and playing the piano—very badly—when no one is listening!

I read a lot too, but don't want to be accused of plagiarism, so when I write, I usually limit mention of my reading to book titles or authors' names!

What Winter Means to Me:

In some ways, I'm not a fan of Christmas – too much commercial stuff and money-making. And the shops start selling cards in *September*, if you please! Meanwhile, the decorations in the town go up far too early, even before Remembrance, which I always feel is disrespectful to The Fallen.

On the other hand, I enjoy sitting in the house, and being cosy when the heating comes on (Hot weather doesn't agree with me, and although I brace myself to receive a larger bill from my energy suppliers, it's easy to forget how much I will owe until the bill actually arrives!).

I love singing Christmas music, especially pieces by classical composers, and I enjoy Christmas food. In my family, we have two Christmases. My sister-in-law is Ukranian and we celebrate on 25th December and again on the 7th January: two very different meals on two very different occasions. And I like buying presents for friends and family.

Cuddling under the duvet at night is wonderful, staying warm with a hot water bottle (or two), and in the daytime, watching the leaves slowly appear on the trees and the flowers grow in the garden...

Terry Dickson

In January 1947, I said hello to the world; it was almost a fleeting visit. Born six weeks premature in what is still held to be the worst winter of the last Century. As I loafed around in an incubator at Edinburgh Royal Infirmary, my poor mum trudged through ice and snow three times a day to breastfeed me. Despite that ordeal, she still went on to care for me.

I went on to become an unremarkable student and failed to clear the academic hurdle of the 11+ exam. Destined for a life of manual labour, I worked doing a repetitive job in a noisy, dusty factory, and that couldn't be my life.

I joined the Army at seventeen years of age. My time in the Argyll and Sutherland Highlanders was an adventure. I served in armed conflicts in various parts of the world. Nine years later, and newly married, I left the army. Unable to settle into various jobs, I was encouraged to join the Police by the Employment Centre Staff. I wasn't sure that it would suit me. However, I did join, and it suited me; I served for 30 years. Twenty-five of those years were as a Detective, dealing with the darker side of our society.

On retirement, I pursued my interest in photography. Studying the concept of Photography as Fine Art, I achieved a Master's Degree at De Montfort University. Having been a keen reader all my life, I wondered if I could learn to write. In 2018, I joined a Creative Writing Class to see if I could learn the craft of storytelling. Continuing with the classes to this day, I still enjoy the challenge and the fellowship of like-minded people.

What Winter Means To Me:
Traditionally, winter is a time to rest, renew, and reflect on our good fortune. We live in safety and security, while many people in the world struggle to survive, putting our often petty concerns

into perspective. Shorter days and longer nights curtail some of our physical activities as we gravitate towards our warm homes. Although grey days when the light doesn't change can be a challenge, more family time makes up for it. Winter is a good time.

Les Dowse

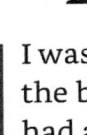

I was born on a small farm in Lincolnshire at the beginning of World War II. By age ten, I had already decided that farming wasn't for me—too hard work, poorly paid, and long hours. Consequently, upon leaving school, I attended University and, with a degree in geology, spent the next six years working as a petroleum geologist in Libya and the North Sea areas. Although liberally remunerated, I had given up six years of social life and shuffled sideways into the water industry as a hydrogeologist to regain a more normal lifestyle.

Over the next fifteen years, I married, had two daughters, earned a master's degree in hydrogeology, and rose to become Water Resources Manager for the Trent River basin— i.e., the East Midlands, essentially. Personal circumstances then forced me to give up full-time employment. I worked as a part-time Map Librarian at the University of Leicester for five years before returning to full-time work as a planning liaison officer with Severn Trent Water, where I remained until my retirement.

Soon after retiring, I started writing — among other short-lived enthusiasms — and found it so mentally rewarding that I persisted and, in due course, enrolled in a creative writing course at the local college of adult education. Over the years, I became one of a group of friends and fellow writers who eventually decided it was time to get something published and set up their own publishing house, "Pen Pals".

Besides writing, my interests include reading —particularly detective fiction — and a wide range of topics, such as wildlife, reincarnation, early human origins, prehistoric aliens, language, archaeology, cosmology, and the fundamental nature and purpose of the universe.

What Winter Means to Me

Winter. The very word is duplicitous. There is no 'win' for anyone in that miserable season. All is lost. Sunshine, warmth, blue skies, dry underfoot conditions, leafy trees and other plant life, birds and animals disappearing with migratory and hibernatory agendas. The remainder of the animal kingdom scurry through the wind-whipped, ice-encrusted, snowbound, flood-bedevilled world with nothing on their minds but survival against the odds until sweet Springtime comes again.

Perhaps one should interpret the season's name as being less to do with a 'win' and more to do with 'inter'. Yes, this is the season of bury or be buried. Bury yourself in a cave, bunker, underground refuge or some other cosy fastness and snooze away the wretched months like those sensible chaps, the bears, do. Or be buried by deluges of rain, snow and mud. This is the season for putting up shutters, battening the hatches, turning up the heating and putting on woolly clothing. This is the time of year to maintain a copious supply of strong drink and comfort food to ensure both one's physical and mental well-being during nature's annual shutdown.

Sheila Mayor

I was born and raised in a little village in Fife, Scotland. In 1970, I made my home in Leicester. I am married to Chris, and we have two sons. Over the years, I gained qualifications in typing and office administration, which allowed me to pursue a career in a training environment and, latterly, work in a children's and family centre. Throughout my career, I have enjoyed working with and assisting people. I follow humanist principles, valuing kindness and helpfulness towards others.

Over the years, we have visited and enjoyed many parts of the UK. We cherish our trip to Kenya, where we fulfilled our ambition to see wildlife, and we made road trips in America with our friend from Connecticut. The coast is special to me; I love walking on the beach and reflecting on writing topics.

Now retired, I enjoy writing and am currently working on my memoir. I read a good deal, take countryside walks, watch wildlife, and spend time with friends. My favourite time is spent with my sons, daughters-in-law, and five grandchildren.

What Winter Means To Me

Winter to me is a mix of emotions. When the trees have shed their leaves, the frosty mornings crisp and clear, I imagine nature getting ready to wrap up and rest for a few months. I am not so keen on the long, dark nights and dread the snow, but I don't have to turn out on a cold morning to go to work now I'm retired. Late autumn and winter are times I love walking, wrapped up against the cold, feeling the crisp air on my cheeks. It is always a pleasure to sit and watch birds on the feeders and at the fat balls in the winter. Thoughts of bonfire night and Christmas time, when our family spends time together, make me happy. Winter gives me time to read more and write. When the snowdrops peek their heads out, I know winter is beginning to wake up and greet spring.

Malcolm Nez

I trained in the sciences, mostly applied sciences, which I used in my work: first in the coatings industry for a few years, and subsequently for forty years in energy conservation. Much of my work was reported in technical style and parlance. I had always wanted to write more loosely and artistically, and upon retirement, I started in earnest by joining writers' groups. Pen Pals, started by our one and only Emma, is a product of such a group.

My writing includes mundane and ordinary stories, for instance, accounts of people watching. Yet I like to experiment with writing high drama, fast-paced action, and gripping yarns. These and anything in between are quite conventional.

Conversely, I am inclined towards the unconventional, speculative, eccentric, avant-garde, and surreal in any combination. I like to view the world from a slightly askew position, observe it thus, and report it as I see it. Moreover, somehow, I can not resist a little buffoonery. None of these is on offer in my contribution to this edition of Pen Pals.

Lastly, I hold a few strong opinions, though not exactly convictions, as I like to seek evidence and confirmation. Then I would like to write something in connection with these opinions. A task for a future edition, maybe.

What Winter Means To Me

The highlight of winter is Christmas and New Year, and my favourite part is carol singing. I have always seen Christmas as the focus, but Scottish friends and relatives, whilst being Christian, err on the side of the New Year. They tend to party right up to the 2nd of January. Yet again, Spanish friends exchange gifts when the three wise men, the Magi, arrived in Bethlehem on the 12th night. So, they will party until the 5th of January.

Those who practice the orthodox religion take it even further. I have Polish friends who are Catholic in religion. If they were part of the Polish Orthodox Church in the East of the country, they would go even further into January, for they have Christmas day on January 7th. So, their party starts when the Spaniards stop. There will be Orthodox Christians married to Spaniards. Just imagine their Christmas.

Pagans celebrate the shortest day, which is generally December 21st or 22nd. It is midwinter or Yule. The decoration of homes with sprigs of evergreen trees probably originated in Yule traditions among the Norse peoples.

My neighbours adorn their windows with brightly coloured lights, which are wonderful, just a month or so too soon, being in late October. Well, too soon, that is, for Christmas. It is always a pleasure to say happy Diwali to them, and a month or so later, they respond with Happy Christmas to me. The triumph of light over darkness, the South Asian festival, is almost what we celebrate in our Christmas.

In the run-up to Christmas, the children write a letter to Santa. Once done, the children take their letters and send them up the chimney, which is just lovely, as the next time the fire is lit, they are burned to a cinder. Written, posted, ignited, toasted, job done. The adult, having taken note of what was requested, then buys it, wraps it and places it under the tree. This seems to be a Scandinavian tradition which we have adopted.

But the earth turns, and from Christmas, the days lengthen by not quite four minutes daily. It is itself a sort of gift. Not really noticeable, but the expectation is there. This increasing daylight will become evident in three or four weeks; nature will not be hurried.

Equally, at Christmas, we are at the end of cool and about to enter cold or even very cold. When mists and damp pavements become clear skies above and frost below, we cannot escape winter's cruel claw drawing us in towards months of hardship. We wonder how people from ages past managed.

The noble's stronghold and his (rarely her) peasants on the land would eke out their stock of kindling for the fire, not knowing how much to keep by for the coming months. Their meat and vegetables, too. There might be much worse to come, or it might be mild. Even now, we have no reliable long-term weather predictions, nor do we know the full workings of Stonehenge. If we can't understand a pile of rocks, then what hope is there?

Personally, I have reached the time of life when winter is not an exciting prospect. When snow is a nuisance or a danger, not a fun thing, not even for modelling snowmen or snowwomen, not for sledging, nor for snowball fights. Incidentally, the difference between snowmen and snowwomen is, of course, snowballs. It is a time when energy consumption and heating bills go up through the roof, as does the warm air we have paid to heat. It is a time when washing doesn't dry either because it's rained on, frozen, or blown off the line. Delightful.

A true delight is the time when all the shops and the malls switch off their jingles, having played them nonstop since September or October. The Christmas switch-off comes not a moment too soon. The relief is palpable. If it weren't for Christ's birth, would we have jingled all year long? Possibly.

Conversely, I do like to sing carols for an hour or so several times a year. Often, there are sweetmeats and hot tea to be had at carol services, which is lovely and all very Christian. It is a time when people practice nearly a thousand years of written music, from monastic chants to frantic, frenetic rock. Which sort of brings us back to jingles again, if not to the very start.

Tony O'Dwyer

I am a retired librarian, formerly with Leicestershire Libraries, and I now study Creative Writing at Leicester Adult Education College. I won a prize for a poem printed in *The Yellow Book*. I am also an artist and have illustrated books for the Private Press. I am a member of the Leicester Society of Artists and the Leicester Sketch Club. I play the clarinet and the saxophone with local Jazz bands.

PEN PAL TALES
a collection by nine
LEICESTER AUTHORS

Tony sketched the central illustrations used on all of our front covers and provided key consultation on the overall cover design. Each Pen Pal Tales book features a unique image offering a different perspective of Leicester, all drawn by Tony. The image shown on the left is from Book One, and the central illustration on the cover of Book Two is also his work. Tony is also an encylopedia of Leicester knowledge, history and creative life, which is valuable.

Maria-Irina Popescu

I am a novelist and story writer exploring the gothic, uncanny, and unsettling aspects of human experience. My novel, *Iridescent,* made the Top 100 of the Cheshire Novel Prize and is being read in full by literary agents. I co-founded *Pen Pals*, a creative network nurturing Leicester's underrepresented literary talent; my story, *The Promised Future,* was published in *Pen Pal Tales.* I completed the first draft of my second novel, *Blackout.*

Originally from Constanța, Romania – once the site of Ovid's exile – I lived for over a decade in Colchester before settling in Leicester. As a non-binary, bisexual immigrant, I write from an intersection of identities that inform my worldview and how I tell stories. I hold a PhD in Literature from the University of Essex, where I researched political violence, Othering, and queer histories. I bring critical rigour and lived experience to fiction that is both intellectually searching and emotionally resonant.

What Winter Means to Me:

Dictator and dictatress in front of
the ginger-bread house.
Blind but not blindfolded.
I raised you all like a
mother, she screams, to hell
with you all but hell's yet to come,
hell's his and hers, holding hands on
the poplar-lined path to
the firing squad.
Scarlet slush yellow slush
and tinsel, baubles, candles

soot-stained slush and mulled wine.
Ice to slide on and frozen stray dogs.
Carols and icicle daggers
stiff with the loneliness of retirees.
Trying too hard to remember
in overheated rooms
what snow feels like.
A rubber bottle leaves blisters
as unmarked graves thaw and
reveal their dissidents.
I unwrap presents.
In another world orphans slip
down in the sewers. Heat pipes
and steam and sniffing glue keep them alive.
It's all the same world but
sewers now lie privatised.
No more freebies for the street rats.
A train snowed in, mid-field,
I'm small and hot and worried about.
Loved.
So lucky so lucky so lucky
I am to look upon winter with
nostalgia's fire-glow. Losses, yes,
losses when the pupil yawns and swallows all.
Damp matches light and choke and
the little matchstick girl is never going home.
I can't keep the sadness down.
Whether it burns or it freezes
this story's ours to swallow.
So lucky so lucky so lucky we are, knowing
it passes. Yes. It passes

Rosemary Watson

I was born into an RC family in Newcastle upon Tyne. Two brothers and a sister were in my family. Educated at a convent primary school, I enjoyed an excellent education that excluded the realities of living in a post-war Britain.

After passing my 11+, I attended an all-girls school where I enjoyed many subjects, both academically and practically. As well as Hockey and watching football, since girls weren't allowed to play, I spent three years in the Newcastle United Supporters Club at both home and away games.

There was no money then to send me to University, so I worked very happily in Edinburgh for three years. My family moved to Leicester, where I met my Scottish husband, and we had three children.

I completed a pre-degree course at Leicester FE and chose to study my BA (Hons) at Northampton. Also PGCE at Bedford, D32, D33 Certificate in Counselling. I worked at Oxford FE and Northampton FE, but after completing TESOL, I worked in Quenca, Spain, alongside a fellow mature student.

I soon went to Madrid for an interview at the British Council, where I successfully worked for two years on a bilingual project, which was a realisation of my dreams and ambitions.

For the remaining years up to retirement, I joyfully lived and worked in Marbella at British Schools, teaching GCSEs and IB. My final school was Las Chapas, an all-girls Catholic School, which completed the circle from my Primary School Days.

Retirement near my children and grandchildren has been active, and I have enjoyed joining the Creative Writing Group in Leicester, where I can 'dredge up' many memories of travel over the years. I have learned new skills and met wonderful people with whom I continue to enjoy a lifetime of learning.

What Winter Means to Me:

Winter is a chance for the earth and nature to hibernate, chill out, take a rest from all the growth and cutting and chopping and not just endure but enjoy the beauty of recharging.

Winter, where my memories drift back to the 1950s, where frozen enjoyments of endless fun are overtaken by the freezing cold reality of one coal fire to heat our home, but we had a liberty bodice then and a resistance to build up.

I was born in December, married in winter, and my babies were all born in winter, so memories of snow and playfulness, as well as endurance — trying to walk on ice while pushing a pram — evoke happiness, not a sense of enduring testing times.

The seventies winters of discontent played out as I grappled with the mechanics of driving a two-litre car and learning to stay on course while going into a skid.

Then came winter travel, and cold and wind and sleet were replaced by more sunshine, throwing the seasons into a strange time of meltdown and unreliability.

The 1980s brought more central heating, greater knowledge of climate change, and an awareness that the world we had taken for granted was no longer viable.

Returning from living in warmer climes to retire, I tend to stay indoors more and pursue hobbies, but to escape to the seaside and for other small adventures that keep me active and enjoy the little people, I still find winter a positive time of renewal and enjoyment.

Emma Astra

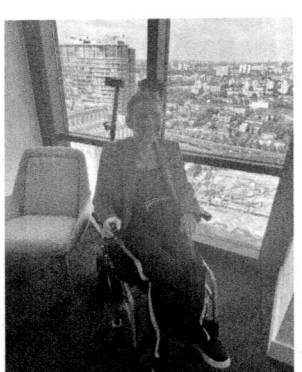

Dr Emma Astra (PhD) is a "Lived Experience Expert," writer, and independent researcher from Leicester. Her writing blends realism and social commentary, drawing on life with chronic illness and disability.

Through the Emma Astra Foundation, she develops inclusive digital storytelling projects such as Leicester Lives and the *Disabled Peoples Project,* and co-founded *Pen Pals Publishing.* These grassroots collectives turn authors' writing into accessible, affordable books.

The photo in this biography was taken at the *Mirror* Newspaper Offices in Canary Wharf, London, in August 2024. Emma Astra has a special interest in raising awareness of people's experiences through journalism, social media and British soap operas. www.linktr.ee/emmaastra.

What Winter Means To Me:

When people ask me, 'Do you like winter?' I say, 'What would I love about cold going through your bones, and just wanting to hibernate indoors?' So, I really should like winter because my favourite thing to do is stay indoors. I am indeed most productive writing from my bed, with the toilet and TV always within view.

So why don't I like winter? I am rather contradictory, really. Because as I was baking hot during last summer, 'I can't blooming write in this heat' was my motto. I even contemplate investing £2k in air conditioning for my "office" (bedroom) one day, not just for the coolness in summer, but also because the units surprisingly give off heat in winter.

I am now saying that the winter darkness is making me tired and unmotivated, and that I am getting up later and missing valuable writing time. The reality is, I, of course, make every excuse under the sun not to write, because creative writing takes vulnerability. Not only to write, but to worry about what others think.

Then I realise that writing is like that period of my life, when I actually went outside — that drunken 3 am sncg in the nightclub. Sometimes you wake up with regret, sometimes it gives you the ick, but if you are lucky, the experience gives you satisfaction. Quite often, though, you or the other person receives the satisfaction, not both.

The best relationships, of course, learn to live with that and experience the satisfaction at different times. Writing, for me, is maybe pursuing that kind of relationship more, like my contradiction of love and hate for winter. The writing may give me or you the ick afterwards, but it does make a learning experience, and a story for your future self.

I recently watched a documentary about writer Fredrick Forsyth. He said he wrote his first book, arguably his most successful, which was turned into a film (The Day of the Jackal) within a month or so of writing it. I saw in another interview he did in an online article by Mark Dapin that Forsyth often wrote ten pages a day for fifty days, then sent the book to his agent, with only a few amendments returned. Although Forsyth says his journalism was a good training ground for accuracy and fact-checking, I can't help but feel his writing/editing technique proved successful. Val McDermid also said during a BBC interview, for a documentary called "In My Own Words", that her journalism became good writing material for her crime stories, but she protected herself from the lawyers by creating fiction from her life experiences.

My New Year's resolution is to be brave enough, like Forsyth, to spend less time editing and more time being more outrageous and proactive in my writing. And, learning from Val McDermid, in writing more fiction like my piece for this anthology, rather than my default non-fiction specialism.

I hope one day we both get that in a balanced, loving relationship between writer and reader. I'm continuing to practice, like I did when in the nightclub all those years ago. Even if we both don't achieve satisfaction, we might have some good stories to share about the experience in a future *Pen Pal Tales* book.

Thank you for reading this book. We hope the collection entertained and even inspired you to try creative writing or read different genres.

Keep updated with our future books and writing at

www.linktr.ee/penpalspublishing

From all at Pen Pals, Leicester, December 2025.

Printed in Dunstable, United Kingdom

74454870R00087